THE OUTCAST SPIRIT
AND OTHER STORIES

LADY DILKE (1840-1904), born Emily Francis Strong, was an author, art historian, feminist and trade unionist. She wrote numerous articles and books on art, in both English and French, and, during her lifetime, published two darkly themed collections of short stories titled *The Shrine of Death and Other Stories* (1886) and *The Shrine of Love and Other Stories* (1891).

BRIAN STABLEFORD has been publishing fiction and non-fiction for fifty years. His fiction includes a series of "tales of the biotech revolution" and a series of meta-physical fantasies featuring Edgar Poe's Auguste Dupin. He is presently researching a history of French *roman scientifique* from 1700-1939 for Black Coat Press, translating much of the relevant material into English for the first time, and also translates material from the Decadent and Symbolist Movements.

SNUGGLY BOOKS

LADY DILKE

THE OUTCAST SPIRIT

AND OTHER STORIES

With an Introduction by

BRIAN STABLEFORD

THIS IS A SNUGGLY BOOK

ISBN: 978-1-943813-13-1

Contents

Introduction

TWO collections of short stories baring the signature "Lady Dilke" were published during the author's lifetime, entitled *The Shrine of Death and Other Stories* (1886) and *The Shrine of Love and Other Stories* (1891). She was attempting to prepare another when she died in 1904, having completed three stories and sketched outlines for five others. Her second husband, the radical Whig politician Sir Charles Dilke, published two of the three that she had completed in a posthumous volume containing her *Book on the Spiritual Life*—both of which are included here, alongside all the stories save two from the earlier volumes.

The two published volumes enjoyed some critical success when they first appeared, although some people disliked them intensely, and even the most fervent admirers of the author's prose expressed anxiety that the stories were so relentlessly downbeat as to appear morbid. Even her friends were somewhat discomfited by their seemingly gloomy nature, in that it did not seem to them to be consonant with her character, which was extraordinarily resolute. There is, however, nothing else quite like them in the annals of English literature, and even readers who have little sympathy with their stylistic affectations, allegorical pretensions and harrowing conclusions are likely to admit that they have a peculiar fascination. Those who find some resonance in their psychological ambience might easily think them touched with genius.

"Lady Dilke," as she was by 1886, having married for the second time the previous year, had been born Emily Francis Strong in 1840. In her youth she preferred to be called Francis, retaining the masculine spelling—she had been named after her godfather, Francis Whiting—and she showed an unusual enterprise and assertiveness in her late teens, when she left home to study at the new School of Art at South Kensington, to the horror of her family but with the active encouragement of John Ruskin. She also had an unusual sense of realism in regard to her ambitions, and when she decided, rapidly, that she did not have the requisite talent to be an artist herself, she diverted her interest into a more passive vein, which eventually made her an art critic and art historian of fearsome expertise.

She developed that diverted ambition with method and dedication after marrying Mark Pattison, the Rector of Lincoln College, Oxford, who was twenty-seven years her senior, in 1861. Although she signed her published work conventionally as "Mrs. Mark Pattinson" she usually signed her personal correspondence "E. F. S. Pattison," deliberately retaining the initial of her maiden name. After Pattison's death in 1884, however, when she married Charles Dilke, she elected to change her name completely, from then on calling herself "Emilia, Lady Dilke," and it was in that new personality and under the signature "Lady Dilke" that she published her fiction and her definitive work on the history of eighteenth-century French art. She had steadily built up a very solid reputation as a scholar during her first marriage, when she had published three books and had been a frequent contributor of criticism and philosophical essays to such periodicals as the *Saturday Review* and the *Academy*, but it was during the second marriage that her most crucial contributions to scholarship were produced.

Much of the critical and historical attention that Lady Dilke has received has focused on incidental details of her two marriages rather than her work itself. The fact that, at twenty-one, having previously shown an independence of spirit unusual in a young woman of the Victorian Era, she married a clergyman of forty-eight, led to some raised eyebrows at the time, and the odd couple achieved a curious oblique fame because her friend George Eliot was thought to have borrowed some elements of the relationship between Dorothea Brooke and Casaubon in *Middlemarch* from her perception of the Pattisons. That assertion was still being repeated in her obituaries, and spurred Charles Dilke to write about it at some length in the memoir of his late wife that he added to *The Book of the Spiritual Life*. Dilke denied that there was any resemblance between the hard-headed Francis Strong and the naively soft-centered Dorothea beyond certain aspects of her religious convictions, or much between the perfectly genuine scholar Mark Pattison and the poseur Casaubon. He also asserted that his wife had told him, in responding to the supposed representation of her in the novel, that she had never read *Middlemarch*, although he plainly did not believe her (Mark Pattison certainly had, and hated it).

In fact, of course, it was not particularly unusual for young women of the time to marry much older men, and not at all unusual for them to marry for reasons that had nothing to do with sexual attraction. Francis Strong married Mark Pattison not because she was passionate about him but because she was passionate about learning, and there was no other practical route to serious scholarship available to her than to be married to a serious scholar. She not only hoped that she could learn abundantly from him and help him in his own work— an expectation that proved far more justified in her case than the fictional Dorothea's—but that the marriage would enable her to enter the society of the Temple of Learning that was Oxford University, and that marital status would allow her to travel for the purposes of the research vital to a historian of European art.

The third element of that expectation was fulfilled, as was the first, but the second proved a frustrating disappointment; although she did, indeed, make the acquaintance of many intelligent men in the University, she did so in a social context that was parochial, small-minded and unbearably, as she put it, "tactful." Even so, the whole arrangement might have worked out entirely satisfactorily from her point of view if Mark Pattison's expectations of a wife had not extended considerably beyond a helpmeet and fellow scholar, apparently leading to deep anguish and resentment when she eventually confessed to him—in a letter quoted by her more recent biographer Betty Askwith—that their physical congress was for her a mere matter of duty in which she had long persisted in spite of a pronounced repugnance.

"Emilia's" subsequent marriage to Charles Dilke, by contrast, was definitely a love match, from which she expected, and proclaimed to all and sundry that she had obtained, an unalloyed happiness. From her point of view, that happiness seems to have been quite unspoiled by the fact that, not long after the marriage, Dilke's glittering political career—he was widely regarded as a potential future Prime Minister—was spectacularly ruined when he was cited as a co-respondent in a divorce case. It is now universally recognized that petitioner cited him falsely, in order to protect her actual lover, encouraged by her mother, who had once been Dilke's lover and was bitterly resentful of him marrying Emilia, but at the time it was marvelous fodder for the evolving popular press, who made the most of it as the scandal dragged on, maintained by a campaign of vilification on the part of the accuser that occasioned further court proceedings. Emilia remained serenely steadfast throughout, but that could not stop speculation about how she might really feel, or prevent subsequent readers of her work from combing her doom-laden fiction for evidence of traumatic fallout of her second marriage as well as her first.

In fact, however, it seems very probable that the content and manner of her fiction had little or nothing to do with the circumstances of either of her marriages, and were engendered and developed from deeper and very different roots. The author expressed mild wonderment herself that she only seemed to be able to write "unhappy stories" during her happy second marriage, and her preface to *The Shrine of Love* offers a rather curious defense of that tendency, which makes the observation with regard to her protagonists that:

"And, looking at such troubled souls, surely one may ask whether sin, like sorrow, has not its own secret sources of purification so that it may read even a higher virtue than stainlessness? Only, in all the ways of life one thing seems ever fatal, one thing alone means always failure, that is the want of absolute sincerity of purpose."

It would be stretching a point to say that all Lady Dilke's stories have for their subject-matter studies of absolute sincerity of purpose, or the want of it, but it is certainly their most vital running theme, and although the purposes of individual characters vary, two elements stand out, often in difficulty or conflict: a quest to love and to be loved, and a quest for some higher or further meaning that might perhaps make sense of the manifestly tragic business of human existence in general.

All the author's other endeavors, at various stages of her life, gave abundant evidence of a determined attempt to maintain "an absolute sincerity of purpose." It is manifest in her scholarly career—and it was no mean feat in an era when the only way for a woman to get into a university was by marrying a don, to establish herself, unquestionably as one of the leading intellectuals in an academic field. It is manifest in the earnest inquisitiveness of her numerous philosophical essays, and, during her second marriage, her ardent and tireless campaigning for women's rights, more than a decade in advance of the explosion of the suffragette movement. There was never anything light or frivolous about any aspect of her endeavor, including her fiction, which is not only earnest and intense to the highest degree but also, and essentially purposive; it is not a reflection of contemporary dissatisfactions but a kind of intellectual and spiritual enquiry into an idiosyncratic aspect of her life that began in childhood and which remained anchored there.

Although it is understandable that Charles Dilke objected in his memoir to the notion that the deep "unhappiness" of his wife's stories was symptomatic of some abiding personal unhappiness on her part that was incapable of any but expression in fictional disguise, there is abundant other evidence to support his contention. There is no doubt that, even at times in her life when she had abundant cause to be unhappy, as when she suffered for many years, during the later phase of her first marriage, from arthritic gout and was often in agony, Francis/Emilia certainly never gave any evidence of it. Perhaps that can be put down to Victorian Stoicism and an enthusiasm for slow martyrdom associated with her undoubtedly strong religious commitment, but if it really had been that, she would surely not have allowed herself to let it lapse so spectacularly in her fiction.

In fact, Lady Dilke offered a very different account of how and why she came to write her stories, which is given considerable support by anecdotal information contained in Charles Dilke's memoir, and which are all

the more intriguing as an account of literary genesis because they are so very unusual—as, of course, would be
required to explain such extraordinary work.

The author had explained to her second husband that
from the age of five or six, she had often suffered from
"hallucinations," some of which involved imaginary
angelic visitations. Unusually intelligent and curious, she
had eventually begun not merely to record her hallucinations scrupulously, but also to seek an explanation of
them. What she meant by an "explanation," however, was
not a religious explanation, or a psychological explanation in the sense that later psychoanalysts might have approached their content, but a physiological explanation.

After being brought up in the Anglican Church, and
then flirting with the Anglo-Catholicism of the Oxford
Movement, Francis Strong underwent a temporary con-
version in her late teens to Comtean positivism. That
was, however, not a lapse from her devout religiosity
but merely a reinterpretation. What attracted her to the
Comtean "religion of humanity" was, in fact, that it retained all the features of Christian religion, with a heavy
insistence on altruism, while discarding the embarrass-
ing mythological elements of dogma. Marriage to Mark
Pattison, obviously, required her to switch back to or-
thodox Anglicanism, but the culture of Anglicanism is
reasonably accommodating to skepticism regarding elements of dogma, and there is definitely a sense in which,
in her scholarly work, Mrs. Mark Pattison and Lady Dilke
remained a positivist; she famously took Walter Pater to
task for the lack of scientific method in is his studies of
Renaissance Art, and dissented from Ruskin on similar

grounds to such extent that he began thinking of her as his arch-enemy, and was quite surprised to learn that she had no personal animosity against him at all. At any rate, it was in that spirit that she tried to anchor her hallucinatory experiences scientifically and philosophically.

Her first conclusion, not unnaturally, was that her visions were partly the product of an unusually vivid and perhaps overactive visual imagination. The second, however, was that she decided, rightly or wrongly, that her two eyes were "of different focus" and that there was a physical peculiarity in the binocularity of her vision that required her to wear spectacles. The note she made quoted by Dilke did not go into further detail—she did not, for instance, suggest that her brain, in negotiating between steams of information that were slightly at odds, sometimes imagined liminal supplements—but the fact that she thought the datum significant speaks volumes about the *kind* of explanation she was seeking for her hallucinations, and makes it far less surprising that her decision as to what to do about them was to put them to practical use as source material for literary works.

In order to do that, she not only recorded the hallucinations, but did so with the specific purpose of developing them in future in a methodical literary fashion. That is why, when she died, she had five stories that were still in the process of development, records of visions or nightmares that were part way through a process of quasi-chemical combination with conscious philosophical notions and controlled stylistic embellishment. Lady Dilke states in the preface to *The Shrine of Love* that each of the stories therein, like those in her first collection, is "a record of the essential facts of some situation which I have known in real life," and that is presumably the key to the process by which she turned the substance of her visions into stories: by fusing them with some circumstance or situation she had observed or experienced, and trying to make sense of the compound by examining it through the microscope of her philosophical and religious convictions.

The same preface offers further indications as to the particular foci of that philosophical microscope, calling attention to the fact that the stories explore the possibility that "those martyrs who have faithfully sought the ideal, otherwise than in he fulfillment of accepted law, whether through a Vision of Learning or at the Shrine of Death, are not wholly accurst," and also explore the "bewildering" workings of "the avenging fates which pursue the mistakes of men" and "the strange coils which form when inherited nature and early training are at war amongst the circumstances of later life." Whether those preoccupations might reflect some deep-seated psychological issues, in spite of their apparent conflict with the apparent satisfactions of Lady Dilke's own life, might still remain a subject for possible investigation, but there is no doubt that they were elements of a conscious narrative method, and a deliberate strategy of composition.

Some of the stories clearly do embody feelings that the author had about aspects of her own life, most obviously "A Vision of Learning," which expresses her deep disappointment with Oxford University as a Temple of Learning, whereas others, such as "The Shrine of

Death" are drawn directly from specific nightmares, but all of them are deliberate alloys, methodically connecting the real with the visionary in a distanced and objective fashion. The visionary element of her work is not necessarily supernatural in the vulgar sense of featuring commonplace supernatural motifs—all the angels, devils and magical objects in her stories are ostentatiously allegorical, and the magicians are mostly charlatans—but it always places the real and the historical within a larger framework that not only contains it but oppresses it relentlessly, with an overwhelming irresistibility, in which ceaseless, inevitable, heart-rending quests for love and altruistic struggles against evil circumstance cannot produce any but fugitive, and perhaps frankly perverse, "secret sources of purification."

The highly mannered style in which that framework is rendered is not entirely without comparison in late Victorian literature. It has some kinship with the quasi-Medieval fantasies of William Morris, whom Lady Dilke must have known, having been acquainted with some key members of the Pre-Raphaelite Brotherhood since her teens and being in frequent correspondence with Edward Burne-Jones while he was associated with Morris at the Kelmscott Press. It also has marked analogies with some of the work done by English experimenters with French "decadent style" such as M. P. Shiel, R. Murray Gilchrist and "Vernon Lee" (Violet Paget), of which Lady Dilke must have been aware, although she would probably have had mixed feelings about it, even though she had stated categorically long before Oscar Wilde that art was neither moral nor immoral, and ought to be assessed purely on esthetic grounds. None of those other writers, however, had her intensity of focus—which, given her stern ideological commitment to the notion of "art for art's sake" and her assertion of the moral irrelevance of art, we must surely construe as a quasi-visual phenomenon, a *literal* intensity of focus, rather than any kind of preaching.

The sources of the style in question are partially revealed by Charles Dilke's observation that his wife's favorite childhood reading was Thomas Wright's adaptation of Thomas Malory's *Le Morte d'Arthur*, which she compared, with her usual analytical attention, with Alfred, Lord Tennyson's "Idylls of the King," whose slow progress she was able to monitor, because Tennyson was one of the many eminent Victorians with whom she was acquainted. Dilke's citation of that analysis is interesting because it reveals her focus on the ideological elements of the mythology of chivalry, dismissing the fighting as uninteresting. Given her initial scholarly interest in the Renaissance and her specialist studies of Eighteenth Century painting, sculpture and architecture in France, the deliberate archaism of her style is surely not surprising. Although there was absolutely nothing "decadent" about her lifestyle or her philosophy of the spiritual life, Théophile Gautier's manifesto for decadent literary style, as well as his manifesto for *"l'art pour l'art,"* must have struck a plangent chord with her. A mock-archaic style is, in any case, uniquely hospitable to allegorical representations of the kind of which Lady Dilke was so fond, and which she found so useful in reshaping the substance of her hallucinations.

It is true that the style of the stories contained in this volume is more likely to seem problematic and uncomfortable nowadays that it would have to readers in the late nineteenth century, who were far more accustomed to such posturing, but there is no doubt that any such difficulties are abundantly compensated by the merit of the stories. The simple fact that they are so unusual is a great asset in itself, from the viewpoint of lovers of exotica, but they are not peculiar merely for the sake of cultivating unconventionality. Seen as an assembly, in fact, their visionary element acquires an extra dimension of coherency, and also manifests a marked evolution, from the slightly tentative experimental ventures of the stories in *The Shrine of Death* to the triptych of masterpieces constituted by "The Hangman's Daughter," "The Triumph of the Cross" and "The Mirror of the Soul," which are truly remarkable works considered individually, but gain even more from being placed in the broad frame provided by this first comprehensive collection of the author's work.

It is not surprising that Lady Dilke chose to title her first collection for "The Shrine of Death," that story being the star item in that initial selection as well as being built around the inspiring spark of the whole literary enterprise. Nor is it surprising that having done so, she should have titled the second collection for "The Shrine of Love," on the grounds that the appeal of symmetry overrode the fact that the item in question was by no means the strongest item of the second set. There is, however, a sense in which the choice of *The Outcast Spirit* as a title for the whole assembly has a particular propriety, because the story-arc and conclusion of that item encapsulate so neatly the uncompromising nature of the visionary frame that contains the whole set of works. It is, perhaps, not a story that can by "enjoyed" in any simple or conventional sense, but it is certainly a story that can be greatly admired, as an encapsulation of the studied world-view of one of the most remarkable writers of her era.

Brian Stableford

A Note on the Texts

We have, in the texts presented here, almost entirely, retained the original spellings, punctuation, and peculiarities of their original publication. Occasionally, however, small amendments have been made. In some instances this was the correction of obvious errors, in others, it has been minor changes in punctuation that it was felt greatly aided the readability of certain sentences. These amendments, however, have been very few and have been kept to an absolute minimum.

THE OUTCAST SPIRIT

AND OTHER STORIES

The Shrine of Death

AH! Life has many secrets!—These were the first
words that fell on the ears of a little girl baby, whose
mother had just been brought to bed. As she grew up
she pondered their meaning, and, before all things, she
desired to know the secrets of life. Thus, longing and
brooding, she grew apart from other children, and her
dreams were ever of how the secrets of life should be
revealed to her.

Now, when she was about fifteen years of age, a
famous witch passed through the town in which she
dwelt, and the child heard much talk of her, and people
said that her knowledge of all things was great, and that
even as the past lay open before her, so there was nothing
in the future that could be hidden from her. Then the
child thought to herself, "This woman, if by any means
I get speech of her, can, if she will, tell me all the secrets
of life."

Nor was it long after, that walking late in the evening
with other and lesser children, along the ramparts on the
east side of the town, she came to a corner of the wall
which lay in deep shadow, and out of the shadow there

sprang a large black dog, baying loudly, and the children were terrified, and fled, crying out, "It is the witch's dog!" and one, the least of all, fell in its terror, so the elder one tarried, and lifted it from the ground, and, as she comforted it—for it was shaken by its fall, and the dog continued baying—the witch herself came out of the shadow, and said, "Off with you, you little fools, and break my peace no more with your folly." And the little one ran for fear, but the elder girl stood still, and laying hold of the witch's mantle, she said, "Before I go, tell me, what are the secrets of life?" And the witch answered, "Marry Death, fair child, and you will know."

At the first, the saying of the witch fell like a stone in the girl's heart, but ere long her words, and the words which she had heard in the hour of her birth, filled all her thoughts, and when other girls jested or spoke of feasts and merriment, of happy love and all the joys of life, such talk seemed to her mere wind of idle tales, and the gossips who would have made a match for her schemed in vain, for she had but one desire, the desire to woo Death, and learn the secrets of life. Often now she would seek the ramparts in late evening, hoping that in the shadows she might once more find the witch, and learn from her the way to her desire; but she found her not.

Returning in the darkness, it so happened, after one of these fruitless journeys, that she passed under the walls of an ancient church, and looking up at the windows, she saw the flickering of a low, unsteady light upon the coloured panes, and she drew near to the door, and, seeing it ajar, she pushed it open and entered, and passing between the mighty columns of the nave, she stepped aside to the spot whence the light proceeded. Having done so, she found herself standing in front of a great tomb, in one side of which were brazen gates, and beyond the gates a long flight of marble steps leading down to a vast hall or chapel below; and above the gates, in a silver lamp, was a light burning, and as the chains by which the lamp was suspended moved slightly in the draught from the open door of the church, the light which burnt in it flickered, and all the shadows around shifted so that nothing seemed still, and this constant recurrence of change was like the dance of phantoms in the air. And the girl, seeing the blackness, thought of the corner on the ramparts where she had met the witch, and almost she expected to see her, and to hear her dog baying in the shadows.

When she drew nearer, she found that the walls were loaded with sculpture, and the niches along the sides were filled with statues of the wise men of all time; but at the corners were four women whose heads were bowed, and whose hands were bound in chains. Then, looking at them as they sat thus, discrowned but majestic, the soul of the girl was filled with sorrow, and she fell weeping, and, clasping her hands in her grief, she cast her eyes to heaven. As she did so, the lamp swayed a little forwards, and its rays touched with light a figure seated on the top of the monument. When the girl caught sight of this figure she ceased weeping, and when she had withdrawn a step or two backwards, so as to get a fuller view, she fell upon her knees, and a gleam of wondrous expectation shone out of her face; for, on the top of the tomb, robed and crowned, sat the image of Death, and a great gladness and awe filled her soul, for she thought, "If I may but be found worthy to enter his portals, all the secrets of life will be mine." And laying her hands on the gates, she sought to open them, but they were locked, so after a little while she went sadly away.

Each day, from this time forth, when twilight fell, the girl returned to the church, and would there remain kneeling for many hours before the shrine of Death, nor could she by any means be drawn away from her purpose. Her mind was fixed on her desire, so that she became insensible to all else; and the whole town mocked her, and her own people held her for mad. So then, at last, they took her before a priest, and the priest, when he had talked with her awhile, said, "Let her have her way. Let her pass a night within the shrine; on the morrow it may be that her wits will have returned to her."

So a day was set, and they robed her in white as a bride, and in great state, with youths bearing torches, and many maidens, whose hands were full of flowers, she was brought through the city at night fall to the church; and the gates of the shrine were opened, and as she passed within, the youths put out their torches and the maidens threw their roses on the steps beneath her feet. When the gates closed upon her, she stood still awhile upon the upper steps, and so she waited until the last footfall had ceased to echo in the church, and she knew herself to be alone in the long desired presence. Then, full of reverent longing and awe, she drew her veil about her, and as she did so, she found a red rose that had caught in it, and, striving to dislodge it, she brought it close to her face, and its perfume was very strong, and she saw, as in a vision, the rose garden of her mother's house, and the face of one who had wooed her there in the sun; but, even as she stood irresolute, the baying of a hound in the distant street fell on her ears, and she remembered the words of the witch, "Marry Death, fair child, if you would know the secrets of life," and casting the rose from her, she began to descend the steps.

As she went down, she heard, as it were, the light pattering of feet behind her; but turning, when she came to the foot, to look, she found that this sound was only the echoing fall from step to step of the flowers which her long robes had drawn after her, and she heeded them not, for she was now within the shrine, and looking to the right hand and to the left, she saw long rows of tombs, each one hewn in marble and covered with sculpture of wondrous beauty.

All this, though, she saw dimly; the plainest thing to view was the long black shadow of her own form, cast before her by the light from the lamp above, and as she looked beyond the uttermost rim of shadow, she became aware of an awful shape seated at a marble table whereon lay an open book. Looking on this dread shape, she trembled, for she knew that she was in the presence of Death. Then, seeing the book, her heart was up lifted within her, and stepping boldly forwards, she seated herself before it, and as she did so, it seemed to her that she heard a shiver from within the tombs.

Now, when she came near, Death had raised his finger, and he pointed to the writing on the open page, but, as she put her hands upon the book, the blood rushed back to her heart, for it was ice-cold, and again it seemed to her that something moved within the tombs. It was but for a minute, then her courage returned, and she fixed her eyes eagerly upon the lines before her and began to read, but the very letters were at first strange to her, and even when she knew them she could by no means frame them into words, or make any sentence out of them, so that, at the last, she looked up in her wonderment to seek aid. But he, the terrible one, before whom she sat, again lifted his finger, and as he pointed to the page, a weight as of lead forced down her eyes upon the book; and now the letters shifted strangely, and when she thought to have seized a word or a phrase it would suddenly be gone, for, if the text shone out plain for an instant, the strange shadows, moving with the movements of the silver lamp, would blot it again as quickly from sight.

At this, distraction filled her mind, and she heard her own breathing like sobs in the darkness, and fear choked her; for ever, when she would have appealed for help, her eyes saw the same deadly menace, the same uplifted and threatening finger. Then, glancing to left and right, a new horror took possession of her, for the lids of the tombs were yawning wide, and whenever her thoughts turned to flight, their awful tenants peered at her from above the edges, and they made as though they would have stayed her.

Thus she sat till it was long past midnight, and her heart was sick within her, when again the distant baying of a hound reached her ears; but this sound, instead of giving her fresh courage, seemed to her but a bitter mockery, for she thought, "What shall the secrets of life profit me, if I must make my bed with Death?" And she became mad with anger, and she cursed the counsels of the witch, and in her desperation, like a creature caught in the toils, she sprang from her seat and made towards the steps by which she had come. Ere she could reach them, all the dreadful dwellers in the tombs were before her, and she, seeing the way to life was barred for ever, fell to the ground at their feet and gave up her spirit in a great agony. Then each terrible one returned to his place, and the book which lay open before Death closed with a noise as of thunder, and the light which burnt before his shrine went out, so that all was darkness.

In the morning, when that company which had brought her came back to the church, they wondered much to see the lamp extinguished, and, fetching a taper, some went down fearfully into the vault. There all was as it had ever been, only the girl lay face downwards amongst the withered roses, and when they lifted her up they saw that she was dead; but her eyes were wide with horror. And so another tomb was hewn in marble, and she was laid with the rest, and when men tell the tale of her strange bridal they say, "She had but the reward of her folly. God rest her soul!"

The Silver Cage

A DEVIL, who was flying through the air one summer's day, grew weary, and spying the roof of a house surrounded by green trees, he directed his course thither and sat himself down to rest on it. As he sat there he heard a sound more lovely than any music, and at first he was so entranced by its beauty that he never asked himself what it was, but by and by, growing curious, he drew nearer to the edge of the roof and looked over into the garden below. There he saw a woman sitting in the sun and sewing a silken shift, and she had hung up her soul in a silver cage on the boughs of an acacia tree over her head; and, as she sat and sewed, her soul sang to her, and the voice of her soul singing of love and of men made enchanting music in the garden.

Then the devil was filled with longing to possess a soul having a voice so beautiful, and he set himself to scheme how he might make it his own. And, looking into the heart of the woman, the devil saw his opportunity, for she had heard the same music from her soul for many years past, yet Love had not come nigh her, and she was ready to think that her soul had deceived her.

So when he saw this, the devil, taking upon himself the shape of a man, went down and knocked at the door of the garden; and the woman, rising and laying aside her work, listened, and asked, "Who is there?" Then the devil made answer softly, "It is one who is fain to enter;" and the woman, who was weary of waiting, said with a sigh, "Is it Love?" But though her soul was still singing to her of his coming there was no hope in her voice as she asked this, for she had ceased to expect him: so, when the devil replied, "Love does not dwell in the hearts of men," she began to muse, and thought, "Perhaps it is even so!"

Then the devil, seeing that he had begun his work, went away and left her to her thoughts; but on the next day he knocked again, and though she did not open to him he noticed that she lingered near the gate. So every day he came back, and every day her lips were less ready with the name of Love, and she lingered longer, listening to the devil's words; but whenever she would have given ear to his wooing the voice of her soul was a reproach to her, till at last one day, when she heard the devil at the gate, she took up the silken shift she had been making for her marriage with Love, and laid it on the cage. Then, the voice of her soul was still, and when its sound was no longer in her ears, she, going down the garden path, heard the echo of her own footsteps and knew that she was alone. Now, when she had asked "Who is there?" and the devil had answered "One who is fain to enter," she said no more, but opened the gate and bid him welcome. So the devil entered the garden, and took possession of the woman, and all that was hers.

As they two went down the borders together, the roses were in bloom and the sun shone brightly, only there was no music in the garden, and at last the devil said to the woman, "Let me hear the voice of thy soul!" So she lifted the silken shift from off the cage and folded it and laid it by, but her soul refused to sing. At this, the devil reproached her, saying, "Shall not thy soul sing for me, since it is mine?" and all the voices outside the garden reproached her also, saying, "Thou thyself hast bidden this one to enter thy garden. All that thou hast is his. If thy soul sing not for him, it is thy sin." Then, the woman wept sore, and by all means she would have persuaded her soul to sing, but she could not, and the devil was very angry and chid her, saying, "This is thy wickedness."

The life of the woman then became so grievous to her that she thought often of Death, and would have embraced him, only he passed her by; and, if indeed she had sinned in opening her gate to one who blasphemed and said, "Love does not abide in the hearts of men," her punishment was greater than her sin. Nor did any give her comfort; her soul was always silent, though she prayed it with many prayers, and the voices outside grew every day louder in rebuke, crying, "Ah! the shameless one, whose soul sings not for him to whom she hath opened the gate."

And the heart of the woman was sore vexed, and, seeing that by no anguish of praying could she induce her soul to sing, she began to work in the garden, watching late and rising early till her strength had well nigh gone from her, and her heart sank. Yet, though in all ways she strove to do the devil service, and in all things she obeyed him, he would not be satisfied since in the one thing she failed, and her soul was always silent. Then, in despair, the woman went out and walked in the miry ways of the world, and she asked counsel of many, and some mocked and some would have found their own advantage in her straits, and others cried "Shame," and bid her keep silence; so that she returned to the garden convinced that the devil had spoken truth when he said, "Love does not abide in the hearts of men."

But it now came to pass that one night late, when she was toiling as one without hope, the woman heard footsteps in the lane without, and one came who knocked at the gate and said, "It is I!" but the woman neither answered nor went, "for this," she thought, "is but one of those without come to mock me." Yet, when the dews fell each night, she heard the same words at her gate, and she began to listen for them, and at the last she believed, and said, with a great sorrow in her heart, "It is thou!" Now, as she said this, she heard once more the voice of her soul singing, and she cried out and said, "Though he may not enter, yet my soul is glad because of him!" And the devil, hearing her say this, was wroth; for the voice of her soul was now so low that its music reached her ears alone, and in his anger he said, "If I hear it not, neither shall thy soul make music for any other!" and, laying his hand upon the silver cage, he opened the door. Then the woman gave a great cry and fell down at his feet, and the devil, putting his hand into the cage to seize her soul, found that it had escaped. Thus, being at the last cheated of his prey, he left the garden, and those without, coming in, found the woman dead; so they put on her the silken shift which she had made for her marriage with Love, and laid her under the acacia tree. And the gate of the garden was closed, and she was left to her rest; but her soul, lying in the bosom of Love, sings for ever in the gardens of Paradise.

The Physician's Wife

L ATE in life a famous French physician took to wife
the daughter of an early friend. The girl herself had
not much to say to the matter; being very young her eyes
were not yet open to the world, so she followed the will
of her family, and went from the north to enter her new
home in the south without doubt or question.

The physician, being wealthy, had wholly renounced
the practice of his art, and had devoted himself for some
years past to the study of certain problems concerning
the origin of life, and in order the better to command his
time he had withdrawn himself to an ancient castle in the
Mountains of the Moors, far away from the haunts of
men. Thither he carried his young wife, and at first she
was not ill-pleased to watch the wonders of his laborato-
ry, and was ready, like a child, to do his errands; but gradually her gaiety forsook her, and her life grew irksome to
her, nor could the disquiet of her spirit long escape the
notice of him with whom she dwelt. Now, in the sight of
this man, Science, pursued for her own sake, was the one
absolute good, and dwelling much with his own thoughts
he had come to be uplifted with zeal, believing that in

truth science had yielded to him the deepest secrets of nature, and that he was thus marked out from all other men.

So it came to pass, that whilst he himself worshipped Science as being the true principle and lamp of life, he demanded of all those who approached him the recognition in him of that deity which, so to speak, should be revealed to them in his person. Nor could any gifts find grace with him, except such as might be brought to render service to that ideal by which his own mind was possessed and in whose name he claimed allegiance from others. He deemed also that he saw all men and all things truly, since, his passions being wholly drawn into the service of Science, he looked upon them without love. Yet, in the number of those who were attracted to him by his fame, there were more sycophants than true disciples, and he knew it not.

When the physician had taken the girl to wife he had looked to have in her a handmaid apt to his purposes, for she was quick witted, and when her fancy was caught by the new wonders which surrounded her in the castle, he praised himself for his discernment, and in the beginning, when her spirit became troubled, he was merciful with her, thinking she was but a child, and by his wonderful tongue he so charmed her ears that she, believing the melancholy which arose in her to be sinful, fought with herself, striving to put the passion of her balked desires into the daily services demanded of her. Her nature was, however, too strong for her will, and her life became very bitter to her.

In the end, there arrived at the castle a new disciple, a youth whom the physician greeted with alluring words, seeing in him one who should devote himself to Science for her own sake; but presently he saw that the youth loved the girl, his wife, and at this he was even less angered than amused, for he thought the passions of youth matters of small moment. Yet, now and again he observed the two, and the girl felt that he watched them. She, however, by this (for she had lived some time under the roof of the physician), had grown to hate the falseness of her life, as fiercely as she had in earlier days chafed against its narrowness. And she asked, "Is it not better to die by any kind of truth than to live in a cheat?" But there was now bred in her the cowardice of the slave, so she gave no outward sign, though her rage and her anguish became greater with every day.

Certain operations were now undertaken by the physician in which he needed the constant help of all those whom he could command, and chiefly that of the girl, his wife, and of the youth whom he had received as his disciple. Nor, being bent on the fulfilment of his plans, would he take heed to all the passion and the pity with which the youth sought to draw the girl to him; she, too, being weary with toil beyond her strength, began to open her heart to him. For at first, when she saw his love, the girl had set herself against it, saying, "Not for this, will I seek freedom, but for myself; since men seek us for themselves alone, and in this they are all one." But now, in her hardest straits, the great love of the youth wrought with her, nor did he leave any means untried which might prevail with her.

So it came to pass one day,—when she had been slow
to follow the physician's meaning and he had chidden her
sharply, and the anger of her heart had leapt to her lips,
and she would have spoken, but again habit had been too
strong for her,—that, he having left them, she, despair-
ing of herself, dazed with long watching and sick with
stifled passion, flung wide the windows of the labora-
tory, and looking out saw the sky grey with rain clouds.
There was an echo of moaning winds in the pine forest
on the hill, and below, mirrored in the still waters of the
white marble basin in the court, the black columns of a
row of ancient cypress trees trembled at the approach
of the coming storm. The girl covered her eyes with her
hands for a moment, and then stretched out her arms
before her. At this movement the youth drew near to
her, and she turning her face, he saw the mute anguish
of her eyes; then, coming very close, he said in a hushed
voice, "You do not know how I care for you!" and the girl
answered, "I do." And there was a great silence between
them.

As they stood thus, the east wind driving from the sea
gathered strength, and seemed as if it would sweep all
the rain-clouds before it; but suddenly there came down
from the mountains a mightier force, bearing in its breast
the very spirit of the storm. Then, in mid-air, far over-
head, the two winds met, and the clouds were caught between them and became a black and awful thunder bolt,
which hung for an instant threatening the earth beneath.
Now was heard a peal at which the walls trembled and
the shutters of every window closed violently, so that all
the chambers in the castle were filled with darkness. In

18

that moment, the youth and the girl sought each other, and their lips met; nor were they conscious of the storm that raged without, for in the soul of each there fell a great calm.

It did not escape the penetration of the physician that there was now a secret understanding between his wife and the youth, his disciple, but he thought, "If she be a fool nought can hinder it. I have shown her the source of all wisdom; if she be unworthy and seek foolishness, let her go. My house shall be well rid of her." And when, as the days went on, he felt that a will was more plainly growing within her which opposed his will, he sought in all ways, by harshness and sarcasm and insult, to drive her forth.

Now the girl, although she bitterly resented this, was cowed, even in her anger, by his tones, so great was her fear of him; and in her doubt she looked to the youth, who was her elder by some years, for counsel. But he, having followed his impulse in striving by all means to win the girl to him, was now afraid of his own work; so, having neither the courage to bid her come out of her bondage and see if they two could face the world together, nor yet the strength to abide in the service of the physician and share her burden, he was already casting about in his mind how he might leave her.

One morning the youth rose full of this thought, and, taking his gun as a pretext, went out to spend the day upon the hills, hoping that in that solitude he might hit upon the easiest way. All the day he passed in much disquiet, planning now this thing, now that, but nothing seemed easy to him, and at sunset he took his way back to the castle, in heavy discontent. As he came down the ravine which led out of the woods, the echo of a song from a band of olive-gatherers fell on his ear, and turning aside from his path he stood and watched them at their work. As he stood thus, the physician's Gift. half forgetting his perplexities, he heard the footstep of one behind him, and at the same time the voice of the physician, saying, "Your luck on my land seems small, young friend." And as he said this, the elder man laughed so that the youth's ears tingled, and he remembered he had not so much as fired a single shot. Nor, in his confusion, could he do more than mutter some unintelligible excuse, at which the physician, having looked keenly at him for a moment, turned away. And, in truth, needing him no longer in his work, the physician would now have been glad to see the youth depart from under his roof.

The youth at this, much shamed and angered, went on his road, resolved now at all risks to tell the girl that he would go, and presently reaching the castle, he entered the armoury, where, laying down his empty pouch and his gun upon the table, he began to pace the floor in heaviness and irritation of mind. To him there came ere long the girl, for she had been uneasy at his long absence, and, seeing the moodiness of his brow, she approached him softly and laid her hand on his arm. But he shook her off, and taking that courage from his momentary anger which he had lacked before, he told her briefly, without disguise, that it was his will that they, at least for the present, should meet no more; and as he marked the whiteness of her face and the bewildered terror of her eyes, he hardened himself, saying that before all on earth his mother was sacred to him, and for her sake he would not abide there, nor could he face her with the girl at his side.

All the blood in the girl's body at this ran backward to her heart, but she did not attempt to gainsay him, only lifting his hand to her lips she kissed the fingers which scarcely closed on hers, and her voice was lost in her weeping. So the youth turned and left her, determined on the instant to leave the castle also. When the door closed on him she looked round her in amazement, as if from the walls there might come an answer to the horrible riddle of her life, and as she did so her eyes fell on the pouch and the gun which the youth had laid on the table. Moving instinctively towards them her foot slipped, for she walked as one in a dream, and as she stumbled she heard the sound of mocking laughter echoing through the window, and looking towards it saw the distorted features of the physician convulsed with malicious merriment. Then, the flood gates of her passion opened and a murderous madness overspread her soul, so snatching the gun from the place where the youth had laid it, she fired on her husband and he fell.

It was soon known that the physician was dead, and that he had died by his wife's hand, but it was agreed that his death should be held to have been by accident. All that had escaped the girl at the time (for she would have openly avowed her guilt) was set down as the ravings of one distraught by a terrible calamity, and she was carried back by her family to the north; nor for a long while would they allow her to be seen by any, but as the years went on they relaxed their guard. Then the youth who had loved her would have married her, but she would not; and he, remembering the passion of her old affection for him, believed, in the vanity of his heart, that she thought herself unworthy to become his wife, seeing that the blood of him who had been her husband was on her hands. This, however, was not in her mind, but her trust in him had died that time when, having striven by all means to make himself necessary to her, he had flung her back to suffer alone; from that day her love had been bitter to her, and when he would have returned her heart was shut against him.

She had reached middle life when she suddenly manifested her intention of going back to the south, and of living thenceforth in the castle which she had inhabited with the physician. For a while those about her sought to combat this resolution, but in vain, and she went back alone, for their entreaties could not prevail with her to let any of her family accompany her, nor did she show any sorrow at parting from them. They all said, "She has never been the same since that day!" Deep in her soul, however, there was resentment against them, for they had all been as one when she had been given in marriage to the physician.

Living through all her last years alone in the rooms in which he had worked, she thought much of him, till she came to see him in a light different to that in which she had conceived of him in her youth. And it seemed to her that though he must needs appear to those whom he sacrificed, one altogether steeped in selfishness, yet his very cruelty arose out of devotion to ends beyond the common aims of men. Then the iron entered into her soul, and she withdrew herself into a closer solitude and silence. And she began to ponder the calculations which had absorbed him; but her brain was now weakened, and refused its service. At last, when long years had passed thus, death, in the mercy of God, came to her. They had watched by her through the night, and morning was dawning, when suddenly she raised herself with a great effort, crying out in a voice of anguish, "It will not come right," and thus she passed away.

By her own wish, they buried her in a nameless grave, and men soon ceased to speak of her story: but not long ago another, whose life was also torture, came to the castle, and, seeing the day dying away in stormy flashes of purple and gold behind the cypresses of the graveyard, entered there. And the tempest in the air spoke to the fury in her soul, so that in wrath and anger she took her way along the darkening paths. "Has any," she cried, "ever borne the like!" and, as she said this, the gusty wind made answer, for suddenly parting the trailing branches of a cassia tree it revealed a tall white cross of wood, bearing neither name nor date, but in the fading light she read the words "Dites-moi un Pater," and above and below she saw drops of agony or tears. Then this woman, awed by the presence of an anguish living beyond the grave, fell on her knees, and when she rose from her prayer, seeing at the foot of the cross a little blood-red flower, she plucked it, and putting it in her bosom went silently away.

A Vision of Learning

THERE was once a boy who was born to all the joys of the South, and day and night he was glad of his life till in his dreams he had a vision of Learning, even as she appeared to men in the lands of the far North. Ever after this he was aware of something wanting to him; at the first, he scarcely knew whether it were so or no, but thenceforth with every hour his need became plainer, till it mastered him, and, turning his back upon the sun, he passed over mountains and rivers, and vast plains teeming with the life of cities, and nothing stayed him till he came to the Northern Sea. There he took ship, and crossed the narrow strait which divided the land in which he was born from that island shrouded in the Western mists, where, as he had heard, Learning held her court.

When he landed, the ghostly wreaths of fog which hang for ever about those coasts arose and embraced him. But, though he felt their kisses on his lips, he was not dismayed, and pressed forward on his way till, after two days' journey, he saw, rising amidst the woods and waters, the towers and spires of that town wherein, as he believed, Learning herself abode. And the people of the town came out to meet him and welcomed him, and when he entered within their gates he marvelled to see the beauty of their city, nor could he praise sufficiently the lordly ways and noble buildings which he beheld on every hand; but at the last he spoke and said: "In which of these palaces, I pray you, hath Learning herself her dwelling-place?" Then all these people answered him as one man: "All these be her palaces, and we are all her servants, and dwell within her walls." And they conducted him within the portals of one of the fairest, and coming to an inner court they led him up many stairs, and opening the door of a little chamber, they bade him welcome once more and left him.

When he was alone he was surprised, for the chamber allotted to him seemed scarcely such as one should have been found within a fabric so splendid in outward seeming; and the staircase by which he had ascended thither had appeared to him very dark, and so narrow that two could not have stood abreast upon its steps; but, in his humility, he deemed it only fitting that one who as yet could scarcely claim to be the least among her servants should find no spacious lodging in the house of Learning. And as he thought these things, looking from his window he saw close opposite to him the grey and crumbling walls of an ancient chapel, pierced with windows of many-coloured glass, and behind the windows he saw lights moving in the gathering darkness, and as he looked he heard voices chanting. And he said with joy: "Lo, day by day every dweller within these walls lifts up his soul in the praise of the beauty of Holiness. When Holiness hath become my portion, and Learning herself

25

hath looked upon me, then shall I have entered into my reward, and shall be as one new-born." So he became a student in that place.

But when many days and months had passed and he saw not Learning, nor even so much as the skirts of her clothing, a great doubt came upon him which made his soul very heavy. After long silence, he spoke to the doctors and teachers and masters and said: "Surely, sirs, Learning hath left you for a space; she hath gone upon a journey, or is holding her court in other lands." But the doctors and teachers and masters were angry at this, crying out: "What strange folly hath possessed you? By whom, then, are our words inspired? In whose name, too, we pray you, do we bear rule over this city? Shall a student who is as yet a dweller but in the outer courts put questions to us?" And they said also: "When you have gotten to yourself all the knowledge of the schools, then may you look to enter her sanctuary." At this the student was abashed, and he thought: "In the days to be, when I have gotten the knowledge of the schools, I shall, perhaps, as these have said, discover her sanctuary."

This was in the summer. Now, though there was no heat in the summer, yet it was very close in the little court wherein the student had his chamber. Often in the evening he would walk in the dusk below his own windows, and on one evening he remained thus walking till it was well nigh dark. Just as he turned himself, thinking that he would go once more within, he heard, on a sudden, a voiceless shriek which filled the air with terror, and looking whence it had come, he saw, perched on the edge of the decaying battlements which encompassed the roof of the chapel, a bird, in shape like to the birds which were common in his own land; but never before had he heard one that cried in such a fashion—a note of warning, of fear, of agony! So standing there white to the lips—for the hideous sound thus breaking upon the silence had shocked him—he watched and listened, thinking that if it should cry again the bird might perhaps utter the low appeals, the idle chatter, and the laughter with which it had been wont to fill the dusk at springtide in the South. But the bird was silent, and presently spreading its wings, soared far away. Then the student longed to follow it, and for a while he believed almost that it had bidden him do so; but at this time the masters praised him, saying he had done well, so he remained.

The summer drew to a close, and the woods lost their leaves, and the rain fell in torrents every day, so that the sky of that country, never very bright, had become an inky grey, and the waters without the walls of the city rose and flooded the adjacent meadows. The student could now no longer go forth beyond the gates, and there were but few dwelling in the inner court where was his chamber, so that when he looked out all was empty and silent, and the windows had that eyeless aspect which gives a ghostly air to uninhabited houses. And, sitting in his chamber, he listened to the perpetual dripping from the eaves, and as the heavy raindrops fell they seemed to smite him, for though he had now gotten to himself much of the knowledge of the schools, and the masters and teachers and doctors spoke fair things of him, yet he knew in himself that he was none the nearer to his purpose.

Sometimes, now, in his weariness he would close his eyes, and for a little space it would be to him as though he trod once more the sunny slopes of his ancient home beyond the seas, and in the breeze the blossoms of the cistus floated as if they had taken wings to meet him in his joy, and all around him there arose the scent of thyme and of lavender and of cassia, and his nostrils pricked with the resinous odour of the dark pines, and he saw their slender columns standing black athwart the silver sky. But when, dreaming thus, he had almost for gotten the vision which had lured him to the North, the dull, metallic echo of the raindrops falling from roof to gutter awoke him, and there was pain in his awaking.

When the autumn was far drawn into winter, it so happened that, rousing himself from one of these fits of stupor—which had now grown common to him—the student went to his window, and looking up he counted, as he had often done before, the lines of a black network formed by the branches of a leafless tree just where the sky was to be seen in a little cleft between the roof of the chapel and that of the court. As he gazed on this, the motionless empty grey of the rain-clouds was stirred as it were by something moving, and slowly, on broad black wings, once more a bird—a bird this time of evil omen—came through the sky and settled down upon the branches.

Then the student thought of that other bird, and half he expected to hear again its cruel note; but this one remained silent, only it ruffled its black plumes and folded its wings. The movement which it made as it did so was like to that made by the doctors and teachers and masters, as they wrapped their robes about them and took their seats in a place of honour, and the student called to mind how many questions he had asked of them, and in vain. Yet it seemed to him as if this bird had a message for him, and knew, perhaps, more than they all of the vision which he had seen in the South. Then he began to be curious about the tree which it had chosen for its resting-place, and in the wildness of his fancy he thought: "If I can but find the place in which that tree hath its root upon which this bird hath chosen her seat, it may be that I shall then discover the sanctuary of which all the doctors and masters and teachers have spoken." But whilst he was still looking on the bird, the snow began to fall, and in a little while both the bird and the tree were hidden from sight.

It now became his chief thought how he might enter the court which lay on the farther side of the chapel, and from which he, like others of his age, had always been excluded; so he went down at night (for not even the snow, which fell heavily, could keep him from trying the adventure) and strove to find some way by which he might pass; but though he succeeded in opening a little iron gate hard by the door of the chapel, he was stopped at the end of the passage into which it led by another which he could by no means unfasten. Night after night did the student continue to essay this second gate, but the fastening was difficult, and there was no light in the sky by which he might have seen how to handle it; the snow, too, lay always on the ground, and the unaccustomed cold was very bitter to him. At last, there came a great storm of wind, which cleared the sky, so that the moon, then in her full, showed forth all her splendour, and on that night the student, when he went down, found that he could open both the gates with ease. So he entered straightway into where there was a garden, only all things were covered with the snow; except where the drift having been swept to one side by the great storm of wind, there was, as it were, a path before him leading into the shadow cast under the farther wall. Looking about, he saw that the garden, like the courts of the building within which he dwelt, was shut in on all sides by high walls, and seeing no issue, he was daunted; when, on a sudden, the bells in an old tower on the farther side chimed with a solemn tolling sound, and there arose an echo of that sound from the other side of the wall, and looking again more steadfastly into the shadow, the student was aware of a little door in the wall, and hastening along the path and coming to it he found it ajar, and pushing it open he stepped within, and knew that he was in a graveyard.

The graves, of which there were many, were all open, and in each there sat men clothed in robes of black or of scarlet, which were strangely bright, trailing in the sheets of snow all dazzling with the moon beams. They were holding with each other high dispute, and the sound of their voices in the frosty air fell on the ears of the student like the echo of passing bells. But he was full of his quest, and after a little pause, going up to the nearest, he said: "Tell me, O master! where shall I find Learning?" And he who sat in the grave shook his head, but he answered not, neither did he lift his eyes. Then the student went to the next, and said: "Sir, tell me, have you seen Learning?" and he likewise answered him not. Then the student turned to a third, and said, with a great agony of praying: "Answer me, I beseech you, have they, the masters, teachers, and doctors of this city—have they seen Learning?" At this all the ghosts shrieked with laughter, crying out: "Neither to them, nor to us, nor to any that have ever abided in this city hath Learning revealed herself." And the sound of their voices crying thus was as the knell of his soul. So the student, seeing at his feet an open grave in which no one sat, asked no more, but saying, "This is my place," he laid himself down in it.

On the morrow, when he was missed, a great search was made for him, nor was it long before he was found. When they had found him they upbraided him with his folly, but he replied: "You are all liars, and now I know you for such; for neither you, nor those that went before you, have at any time seen Learning in this city; the dead have spoken, and have put you to shame." At this all the doctors, teachers, and masters declared: "He is mad." So the student was bound hand and foot, and they carried him to a mad house, and there, because he was very violent, they put chains on him, and the reproaches of his ravings were very terrible to hear, and by no means could the wrath of his tongue be appeased.

For many years he remained in this state, but by chance there came a woman who felt great compassion and sorrow for those in suffering and in bonds; frequently she visited the mad-house, and brought at the least some word of calm or look of pity to the afflicted. It was a long while before the keepers of the house would suffer her to speak of approaching the student, for they feared lest evil should befall her from his great violence.

In the end, however, she persuaded them to take her to him. And they said to her: "Should he ask you if you be Learning, then you will do well, perhaps, to humour his folly, and to make answer that it is even so, and that you indeed are she."

So, bearing in mind their cautions, the woman entered the student's cell, and on the instant, even as the keepers of the house had foretold, he asked her if she were not indeed Learning herself come to visit him. But she, seeing him so all distraught and well nigh dead for Learning's sake, was filled with a yearning of grief, and, forgetting all their cautions, she cried out: "God forbid, my poor lad! I am but Love." And at these words the student began to weep bitterly. Then the woman, without speaking, took from her bosom a red rose and put it in his fingers, and the student, taking it, made as though he would have carried it to his lips; as he did so his chains rattled loudly, and lifting his skeleton arms to heaven, he seemed once more about to call down curses upon men, but the scent of the flower changed his purpose, and he turned his face to the wall in silence.

Then the woman prayed that his chains might be taken off him, and before she left him she had prevailed, and this was done; but on the third day, when she returned to know how he did, she was told, "He is dead," nor could she learn the place of his burial.

The Black Veil

THERE is a village in Norway which stands in a
plain near a lake, not far from the mountains, but
far from the sea, and equally far from any city. In this
isolated spot there once lived a couple of ill-fame; they
were evil to each other, and to all the world beside. He
was the stronger of the two, so she suffered the most;
and the more she suffered, the more her will to repay evil
with evil grew within her, till at last one night she slew
him. But she did not grow strong with her crime; she felt
the shame of it; so even then, when she could say, "I am
free," nothing seemed well with her, and a fear came on
her lest the neighbours should know or should suspect
her guilt.

So he was buried, and she bemoaned him, and she
bought for herself a veil of mourning, longer and thicker
than common. This veil, which was cumbersome at first,
grew day by day more cumbersome, until, when some
months had passed, it was so long that it trailed behind
her, and so heavy that it weighed her to the ground, and so
thick that she could see neither the sun, nor the moon,
nor any stars. And day by day her fears grew heavier, and

her thoughts were ever, "How shall this my veil be shortened; how shall it be lightened; and how shall my eyes be cleared?"

Some of the people then said, "It is her over-sorrow has angered the spirits of the mountain, that have sent this curse upon her." She herself looked towards the mountains, where afar off there dwelt a wise woman, and when the others said, "Go, ask counsel of the wise woman of the mountain," she went.

It was a weary journey, but at last it was done, and she stood before the wise woman, and said, "How shall this my veil be shortened? How shall this my veil, which is heavy, be made light? How shall this my veil, which obscures all things, so that I see neither the sun, nor the moon, nor any star, be made clear to my sight?

Then the wise woman, after a pause, made answer, "Go; pray three times in the night on the grave of him who is no more. Go; pray three times in the night on the grave of him who is not here. Go; pray three times in the night on the grave of him who lies in the earth."

With this answer she went heavily back to the village, and they met her eagerly and questioned her, but she made no reply, for she shrank from the task set to her, and she shut herself indoors and thought, "Peradventure if I go not over the threshold it will be a less weighty burden." But it was not so, and outside the neighbours watched, for they marvelled more and more.

At last, one night of thick blackness covered the sky, and the woman arose and said, "If I go forth now none will see me; here I can sit no longer." And she went forth and betook herself to the churchyard, but she was not alone, for the neighbours watched, and when they saw her go forth they followed her. And she heard them behind her, and turned in fear and anger, and saw that they pressed on her close. Then she made haste, and, coming to the high gate in the wall of the churchyard, she entered quickly and made it fast, so that none should disturb her and play the spy, but she trembled with a great fear, and the darkness was so thick that it stifled the words on her lips. But, at last, they outside heard her pray, and they listened, and there was silence for a space—silence till, with a great cry, she said, "Help me, O friends and neighbours! He drags me down; he holds it, and draws me to him!"

And they outside shook the gate, but within she had made it too fast for all their strength; and she said, "I cannot pray. He draws me! I am going down into the earth!" And her voice grew fainter, and they shook the gate like madmen, and some strove to climb the wall, and when they paused for an instant to listen, all was still.

When the day came, and the gates were broken, and they had come to the grave, they saw nothing; then with frenzied hands they laid bare the earth, and they found nothing, and next they opened the very coffin itself; the dead man was there alone, but in his hand they found a piece of her black veil clutched fast within his fingers.

The Secret

THERE was an old town built on the two sides of a broad river, and on the bridge which spanned the river, and united the two halves of this old town, there stood every day a little boy. He stood always on the upper side, looking to the north: sometimes he looked beneath, and his eyes fell on the waters driving past him, eddying and curling in the piles below, and sometimes he lifted his eyes to the distant mountains. If any spoke to him, he had but one word for them, "Whence does the river come?" Then some laughed, and some said jestingly, "Whither does it go?" and some shook their heads and said, "The child is mad." They drove him to the school with the others, and he went, but still his thoughts were on the bridge, and thither he returned when the books were shut and the door closed. He grew older, yet no joys of youth, no glories of the sunset or the sunrise, no radiance of the south could win his eyes from the cold white light beyond the frozen mountains, and still on his lips there lay ever the same questions, though silence became a closer friend to him with age. Then, at last, he looked his question only, and one drew near and said, "Seek the bosom of the Snow-maiden; the secret is hers, and hers alone."

So visions of the Snow-maiden visited him in his dreams, and all the day was dull to him, and the night when he might see her, if but in sleep, became dear. And the mother who bore him, watched him, watched him with a terrible foreboding, for said she, "My son's soul is lost to me, and his eyes see me not, and his spirit is gone forth, let God say whither!" Then, after many months had passed, she missed him from his bed and she sought for him on the bridge, nor was he there, nor was he any where; and bitterly she said, "He is gone, the child of my womb! nay, not one kiss hath he printed on these lips in token of farewell!" and she covered her face. But the neighbours upbraided him for a vagabond. But the mother said, "Good women, my son is no vagabond; it is the charm of the Snow-maiden that hath drawn him from me."

Meanwhile, he had gone on his way; the river was his companion and his guide, but the mountains were distant, and often the waters lay as if in sleep: then his heart sank within him, for the cold light which told him of the far-off presence of the Snow-maiden seemed to be withdrawn into the recesses of the sky, and the river mirrored the trees and the fields, and even the habitations of men. Still he held on, and when sleep came, and the weariness of despair, then often was he visited by dreams, and the Snow-maiden stood before him and smiled, and he was lost in her beauty. In the morning, he would arise after seeing such a vision, free from the stains of travel, unheeding the dangers of the way, and with all fatigue vanished from him. And as he drew nearer and nearer to the mountains, though his body grew weaker, and he was well nigh to death, then the visions which visited him in sleep were more radiant than before; nay, each one seemed plainer and more evidently true, and he would wake, having tasted the breath of the Snow-maiden and seen her loveliness in all its glory: yet one thing was strange to him, though she smiled on him she saw him not, for her eyes were always closed.

A great passion now woke in his heart, for he said, "If I may not see her eyes, I had liefer die!" and he cried now day and night on her name, for he had reached the mountains, and the rocks were hard to his feet, and his weary limbs would scarce bear him forward.

Then, one night, when the anguish of longing and despair had well nigh slain him, he saw before him a great cavern. He had sunk to the ground in the anguish of his crying, when he was aware of the black cavern before him, and was aware that she, the Snow-maiden, was there. She stood in the entrance, and he dragged himself on his knees to her feet, and she laid her arms about his neck, and he heard her voice. "Art thou come?" she said. "Art thou come at last, O my love, for whom I have waited so long!" and she drew him to her and raised him in her snowy arms, and they entered the cave together. But he was like a man in a trance, and he uttered not one word. Then she wooed him with lovely sayings and signs, and he lay in her arms, and the pure snows of her embraces were upon him, but still he spoke not, and his eyes were as the eyes of one who sees not.

But, at last, he lifted his face to hers, and he looked on the Snow-maiden, and her eyes were still closed, and all the agony of his longing came upon him, and he cried, "Oh! my love, if I see not thy eyes what good shall my life do me. Open thy eyes, my love! open thy eyes, that their light may fill my soul!" Then the Snow-maiden opened her eyes, and in that glance he knew all the ecstasy of love, and his soul fainted within him, and a sound of many waters was in his ears.

Meanwhile the mother was desolate, but one day she ceased moaning, and said, "Come with me, O good women; this day shall my son return to me." And they went with her and they came to the bridge, and when they came to the bridge, the mother turned and led them by a steep path down to the water's edge, and lo! it was so. Her son had come back to her; the waters had brought him from the home of the Snow-maiden: she had taken his life, but he knew her secret, and the light of her eyes was in his.

The Serpent's Head

IN a castle by the Northern Sea two women, a girl and her mother, dwelt alone; nor, had they wished for friends and neighbours, were there any to find in that desolate country. All the space which was not covered by water was spread with sand, for the hills near the coast, mined by the stealthy advances of the sea, were for ever falling over and strewing the shore with ruin. The only feature of this mournful landscape was a black reef of rocks to the north, the position of which was marked, even at the highest tides, by a crag called "The Serpent's Head."

The castle itself, which was on an eminence completely isolated from the surrounding country, showed but the scanty remains of its ancient glories; the great tower yet stood on the north proudly intact within the inner series of fortifications, but facing it on the south and east were nought but ruins, whilst on the west a disused building called "The Chamber on the Wall" presented a gloomy and deserted aspect. Such life as yet lingered within a fortress meant to contain a thousand men was apparently confined to the tower, and centred on the existence of two women.

In a vast and vaulted chamber, the sides of which were riddled with strange closets, and mantled with books, the mother constantly sat; but her gaze was more often on the deserted courts below than on the pages before her, and oftenest of all her eyes would seek the black reef on the north, and spy out the antics of her daughter, diving and swimming about the Serpent's Head.

The girl, in her childish days, had been content, finding infinite amusement, as the fisher children did, in the wonders of the sands; in the hollows of the great drifts she had built for herself many a fairy chamber; but as she grew older these sports were all outworn, and of all her delights one only remained to her, for she was a fearless swimmer, and to dive into the deep waters off the Serpent's Head was ever a pleasure to her.

There, too, she would sit for hours gazing seawards. No tiniest speck of sail that crossed the waters could escape her watchful eyes, and as she watched she dreamed that some day one of these distant sails should bear down towards her, and one should come, in whose hand she would lay her own, and they two would flee to the far East. But as the changeless years went by and brought him not, the girl grew sullen, and a sense of wrong possessed her, for the older she grew, the clearer became her consciousness of a world beyond her, and the greater her longing to seek it.

So the sea, with its journeying ships, appeared to her as the path of deliverance, and the way of escape, and the castle in which she dwelt was as a prison to her; and sometimes sudden fits of gusty passion would overtake her, for weariness grew to hate, and hate to wrath, and rising to her feet she would clench and shake her impotent hands at the grey walls above her, frowning motionless at the ever-moving sea. Then her mother, if by chance she saw these demoniacal gestures, would smile a bitter smile, and when they met her eyes would have a challenge in them, so that the girl's passion, which the moment before had risen high with questioning, fell before her gaze, nor did it ever seem possible to her to speak her thoughts, and there was never any confidence between them.

Thus it was that the girl went always alone, and one morning in the late autumn, having risen from a bed fevered with evil dreams, she betook herself, as was her wont, to the Serpent's Head. It was low water, and stepping lightly from point to point, she soon reached the utmost projecting crag, and sat herself down upon it. Now as she sat, she looked into the waters below, and her eyes fastened on two long ribands of seaweed which floated out of a cave beneath, or were sucked back as the tide ebbed or flowed. As she looked on them, these ribands of weed seemed to her like two long arms stretching and reaching out to her. Then suddenly she remembered her dream, for in her dream it had seemed to her that her own heart lay in her hands, and as she held it before her, lo! two arms had stretched themselves out of the darkness, and her heart lay no longer in her own hands, but in those of her mother, and she heard her mother's voice saying, "It is mine!" and a great anguish had come upon her, as she felt her mother's fingers in her heart-strings, and she awoke.

42

Now when the girl remembered her dream, the fever of the night ran yet in her veins, and she continued to watch the witch-like movements of the weeds upon the water, until it was as though she felt the clasp of their slimy tendrils drawing her downwards, and yielding to a sudden impulse, she sprang to her feet, cast her garments from her, and hastily girding on a little blue gown which she had brought with her, she threw herself into the sea. Once she had touched the water her dream faded, and she forgot her meaning to enter the cave below, and struck out from the land. Nor was it long before all the blackness in her heart vanished, and she began to laugh, joying and sporting in the boundless waters. But soon there arose a sea fog such as afflict those coasts, and in a moment the shore and the sea were as one, for on all sides the impenetrable mist had fallen.

At this the girl made, as she thought, for the point whence she had come, and she did not discover that she had utterly lost her bearings till the sound of the signal, fired from the Castle walls, rolled past her through the waves of shivering mist. She was now weary, but the sound was no sure guide, for, having reached the shore, she found herself still so far out of her course that her feet were in the quicksands which lay to the south of the Serpent's Head. Now anger and fear laid hold upon her, for the tide was coming in fast, and she knew that no man might land at that point with his life; so, turning to the north, she struck out again for the rocks, and the old fever mounted to her brain, and she fancied that the hand of her mother lay heavy on her life, and her thought was, "I will not die, but live. I will be stronger than thou!" And even when, in her extremity, the end seemed very close to her, the fog began to lift, and before her she saw the black shape of the Serpent's Head. Then, with a desperate effort, she drew near it, and the fog lifted altogether, and she saw that no other part of the reef was visible; but though she laid her hands upon it, the numbness of her body was such that she could get no footing, nor by any means could she raise herself on to the rock.

There was one, however, who now watched her, one who had ridden from afar, and caught by the fog and the rising tide had tarried near the rocks. When this one saw the girl clinging to the Serpent's Head, he rode his horse a little way up the shore, till he could put him in the curve of the breakers, and thus, like one who had often done the same, he strove to reach her; but by this means he could not, so next, letting go his horse, he made himself ready, and fetching a wide circle, he reached her and brought her safely to land.

When he touched the shore he laid her on the sands and knelt beside her, and she, half conscious only, opening her eyes and seeing him thus close, made one of her dreams and of her escape from death, and putting her arms about him said, "I have saved my heart, and it is yours;" and she thrust her mouth to his and she kissed him. After this she lay still as in a swoon, and he was amazed; but the girl was very beautiful, and great pity and tenderness possessed him as he saw her thus. Then he looked about for help, and so looking he espied a narrow path embedded in the grass grown sand, and leading to the postern gate of the castle. Taking her then in his arms, he bore her slowly thither, for the way was steep, and pausing now and again he felt that the pressure of her arms about him tightened until she held him so close that when he had brought her into the presence of her mother scarcely might her stiffened fingers be unclasped from about his neck.

Now when at last she opened her eyes, she lay in her own room, and her mother stood near, and she heard her mother say, "Would God that she had perished in the sea!" and she saw her mother's face that it was very stern as she said this. But the heart of the girl was glad; she felt neither fear nor anger, and hate seemed harmless, so great a love within an hour past had leapt up within her. And, though no word had passed, she knew that he who had fetched her from the sea was her lover, and that even as it was with her so it was with him.

Next day, and each day after, they met again by the Serpent's Head; but her mother watched her, and looking towards the rocks at sunset she saw them together. Then neither that night nor the next did she take any rest, and on the morning of the second day, when the girl would have gone forth, her mother met her and said, "I have somewhat to say unto you." And the girl, suspecting her purpose, stood still before her, and folding her arms across her breast she answered, "He is my lover, and shall be my husband." And the mother at this cried, "Are you hot so soon? But I have that to tell you which shall put out your fires. There is a curse on you, even the curse of your accursed father and his race. O God!" she continued, "shall not one life suffice, and shall his seed drag yet another and another down into the abyss? Shall a son born of your body live to rivet these devil's chains on another life as fair as mine?"

And a great shiver passed over her, and she closed her eyes a space before she spoke again, and then it was in a different tone, a tone of pitiful pleading, that she said, "Child! for the sake of your love, put him from you; die sooner than bring this death to his soul;" and in so saying she averted her eyes, for she knew that if she looked upon the girl and saw in her her father's features, the dregs of hate, grown cold, would be as gall within her, and turn her words to bitter. So laying her hands on the hangings of the wall her lips moved silently as in prayer, and she went on, as one in a trance, "I gave my soul to him who was your father, and here for years I served him, but by no service could his spirit be appeased, and the hour came that I knew him to be mad, and he knew it also, but the world knew it not, and a great fear came upon him that I who knew it should betray him. Day and night he watched me, nor could I by any means elude his cunning, till at the last he had me at his will."

Here her voice dropped and her lips were white, as thrusting aside the folds she pointed to the stains on the floor beneath. "There," she said, "is my blood;" and letting go the curtains she loosened her gown and showed a deep and ugly scar upon her breast, and even as she did so, a dagger, dislodged by her sudden action from among the weapons on the wall above, slipped from its holdings and fell between them with a terrible rattling sound. So she stooped, and picking it up looked steadfastly upon it. "It is the same," she said. "Ah, God! that night, and the long days that went before, and the long years that have followed after! Is there any mercy or any justice in Heaven?"

But the girl put no faith in her, and the thoughts which had been in her mind that day when the fog had fallen on the waters returned to her, so that she gave no heed to threats or pleadings, and the anguish of the other's soul moved her to scorn only and laughter, for the story of her house was as a fable to her, and when her mother called on her to stay the curse, and stretched out her hands in her praying, she called to mind the witch-like moving weeds below the Serpent's Head, and she remembered her dream, and how she had felt the fingers of her mother on her heart. Then too she remembered how she had been delivered in her need, and turning to go she answered, "I will not die, but live. I will be stronger than thou."

But the mother said, "Not so; yet if you will do this deed you shall first ask your father's blessing;" and as she said this she laughed, and the girl felt that her laughter was more to be dreaded than any threats.

So now they two went forth, and crossing the court, came to the broken flight of steps which led up to the Chamber on the Wall. When they had mounted these they stood before an ancient door heavily bound with iron. Then the mother knocked, and was answered, and entered, and the girl, though she was stricken with fear, followed her in silence. But when she had come into the presence of her father a great compassion filled her heart, and her eyes were drawn to the subtle appeal of his. "Has she told you," he said, "that I am mad? I am not mad, my little child, it is she;" and here his voice took on an accent of infinite pathos; "it is she, who was once all the world to me, who has abandoned me and left me desolate. Ah! for God's sake take me home! Come back to me, my wife! Give me love! Yet, how should any love such as I am?"

And as he pleaded thus, turning from one to the other, the girl, seeing his chains, thought shame of her mother, and with reproach on her tongue she made to go forward as though she would have embraced him. But her words died on her lips, for looking on her mother's face she saw that it was as the face of one inspired, and even as she was about to advance towards him, her mother put her on one side, and saying, "Lord God! take my life if by this means it is Thy will that this plague be stayed," she put herself within his reach, and kneeling down close to him folded her arms on her breast. Then, before the girl was aware of his purpose, he had her mother in his grip, and before any aid could come near she was dead.

All that night long the girl watched alone by the body of her mother in the tower, and a great struggle went on in her mind as she began to see the meaning of her mother's act, and at daybreak the spell upon her was so strong, that as she saw the grey light of dawn she rose, and falling on her knees beside the bed she folded her arms on her breast, and it seemed as if she, too, were about to dedicate her life that so the curse of her house might be stayed. But the chamber windows fronted the east, and even as she lifted her face to heaven the first rays of the morning sun flushed the sky, and caught the crests of the waves, and the path of light on the waters went by the Serpent's Head and changed its black to

48

gold. At this sight the girl started to her feet, and throwing wide the windows, "I will not die!" she said. "Is there no other way?" Even as she asked this question she answered it with another. "Why should my seed live?" and as she spoke thus, turning to leave the room she saw her own face in the glass, and it was as the face of her father. Then her gaze became fixed, and presently she whispered to herself and smiled. And turning her back upon the corpse she went swiftly to seek her lover on the rocks.

Not long after this the father died, and the girl married her lover, and the castle, which had so long seemed like a vast and empty shell, overflowed with life. And all things prospered with her, only of all the children born to her not one lived. And many said it was best so, seeing that their inheritance, all fair to outward seeming, had so dark a spot within; but the husband was ill content, for most of all he desired a son that should bear his name, and his wife was angered at this, for she thought, "Why should not I be sufficient for him? What need has he of child or heir when I am near?" And her passion for him was spiced with jealousy, and when once more she became with child and saw the hope in his eyes, she set herself to cheat it. Nor by any means could she be persuaded to value rest, or to live in such wise as was deemed fitting; and now at dusk the hoofs of her horses would be heard in mad gallop along the causeway, or at early dawn she would be seen battling with the crested waters off the Serpent's Head.

Between her and her husband there were high words, and he reproached her, and swore that there was purpose in her folly; then she caught him and held him, crying, "Why should this devil's brat come be tween us! You are all the world to me. Am I less to you?" and she would have kissed him, but there was that in her passion which filled him with loathing, and thrusting her from him he said, "Are you mad?" After he had said this he repented himself, but she answered him nothing, only her face blanched. And from this day forward she was very gentle, nor did she cross his will in any way, nor even once did she return to the Serpent's Head; only sitting in the tower chamber there, where her mother had so often sat before her, she watched the waves beating on the rocks. And her husband, wishing to feel her mind, said, "The day will come when you will be there again;" and she smiled as she answered, "Ay! the day will come."

Yet, though she was so gentle, he felt that there was wrong between them, and when the child was born his great joy was poisoned by fear lest it should displease her, and he watched to see if there should be any change in her manner or in her look; but he could find none, till one day he, having taken the child in his arms, looked up suddenly, and thought he saw a gleam of malice in her eyes, yet this faded into smiles so swiftly, that after, when he recalled her look, he misdoubted that which he had seen.

Shortly after this she and her child were missed from the castle, and it was late evening; so fearing he knew not what, the husband looked from the windows to the rocks, and there he descried her, seated on the Serpent's Head, with her little one on her knee. The tide was coming in fast, and dumb with anguish and terror, he made haste to reach the shore; but the way seemed long to him, and even when he drew near to her he scarce dared to approach her, for his fears shaped themselves as he ran, and became one agony of terror for his child's life, and he thought, "If I come upon her unawares, she may cast him into the sea." But she, though her back was turned to him, was aware of his coming, and she rose to her feet and faced him, still holding her child in her arms, whilst he, wading, and often slipping and stumbling, made his way slowly to her.

And as he drew close he saw that she wore the little blue gown in which she was wont to bathe, and her golden hair was loose about her neck as when he had seen her first, and her feet were bare, and a smile was on her face as she kissed the child in her arms as if it were very dear. Then calling and moaning out to him she cried, "My mother's hand is heavy on me; oh! my love, save me! Her hand is heavy on the child, and her arms are stretching from the waves to seize us. Ah! my love, save us!" And now he had almost laid his hands upon her, when she, thrusting the little one from her, shrieked, "Take your devil's brat, I will have none of it!" And he saw that his child was dead.

At this, he made as though he would have seized her, but before he could lay hands on her she had him by the throat, nor could any strength of his avail to unloose her fingers; as he struggled with her thus, he felt the crag rock beneath his feet, and between his teeth he cursed the day that had brought him thither to mix his blood with that of her demon blood.

51

But neither to curse nor to pray could then avail him. The tide came on, nor was there any help from land or sea. And the great waves leapt high above them, and her fingers tightened on him, and her lips clung to his mouth, so that gasping for breath he stamped in his fury with his foot. Then was the great crag loosened utterly from its hold; for a moment it hung above the abyss below; next, with a steady roll and a sound as of thunder, it plunged into the seething waters. In the gathering night a cloud of spray arose to heaven; then the waves rolled on to the shore, and neither in ebb nor flow can any man find where the Serpent's Head has made the grave of its ghastly burden. But the plague of that house was stayed in the land.

The Voyage

IN a shining garden by the sea a fair woman sat desolate, since he whom she loved must needs obey a
summons, bidding him to a distant journey; and she
thought, "How shall I bind his soul to mine, so that he
shall come back to me even as he goes—mine body and
soul?" For these two loved each other exceedingly, so
that no mortal power could have prevailed to separate
them, but the woman living constantly by the sea knew
its witchery, and she feared the magic of the waves and
the marvels of the great deep.

Even as these fears came thick about her, she heard
the footstep of her love, and looking up, she saw his
shadow lying black athwart the sandy path between the
great aloes of the entrance-way; so rising, she went to a
little swing gate set in a thicket of pink roses, and opened it and let him in. Then, lifting her eyes to his, she saw
that the hour had come. The man was moved, and the
woman, clasping her arms about him, put her lips to his
lips, saying, "Go, and bring back to me my kiss!" And he
answered her and said, "Dear, thou knowest no human
power can part my soul from thine!"

So the man took ship and went down to the great waters, bearing sorrow in his heart.

Now, as he journeyed out into the deep and utterly lost sight of land, his past fell away from him, and the charm of the sea and the sky was upon him and grew, so that it seemed, before many days were past, as if he knew no other country; the earth herself had become to his sight but a rolling ball of waters, flying ever beyond the sun, as the clouds closed and fell with every falling day. And as he forgot his past, so did he gradually lose thought for the future, till at the last it was so, that should any have come to him and said, "This is henceforth thy world, this ship on its far journey holds thy fortunes, and beneath its spreading sails shalt thou abide till night closes on thy life!" he would not greatly have marvelled at so strange a tale.

Night by night the voyager watched the stars of heaven, and learned the times of their rising, and knew them by their names; often, too, he sat in the very path of the moon, till the rippling waves of her light flooded his soul, with a silver calm. And, at these times, he withdrew himself from the ship's company, and would willingly be alone. For it seemed to him as if voices of delight were upon the waters in the night watches, only when men spoke with him their loveliness faded away.

Thus, watching and listening, it came to pass that one night, about the rising of the Pleiads, and whilst the Cross yet was lying far beneath the waters, a voice fell on his ears, which enthralled him and brought a strange joy to his heart; a joy not unmixed with pain, for it waked echoes of remembrance, and he recalled that beloved one's voice, the tones of which had been dear to him in the garden by the sea, and he saw her standing silent in her sorrow and looking out beyond the roses, beyond the pale green belt of guardian aloes to where the blue and radiant waters washed the silver sands. Then, two voices began to plead with his spirit, and, hearing as it were in a dream the voice of his love entreating with that other voice of strange music, the man strove with himself, and cried out upon her, and sought to have a yet clearer vision of her beauty, but in vain. The echo of her tones grew faint, the voice of mystery filled his ears, and, even as he strained his eyes, thinking to see her very face, a fair mist, born of the sea, arose and veiled his sight.

As soon as the early dawn had driven all clouds from the face of the morning sky, the man came to himself; but he was very moody, and this moodiness increased upon him throughout his journey, and he lived through the day watching only for the sunset, when there sprang up a light breeze, and with it the expectation that in the night watches he should once more hear the voice of music, and shroud himself with the mantle of the fair mist. And when he received letters from the woman whom he loved at the port for which he was bound, the tale they told had no meaning for him, and he made haste to go again on board: not that he had any desire or longing to the garden wherein she sat, but rather that he felt haste and impatience to dream once more his dream upon the waters.

Now when seven times seven days had passed since that hour in which he had gone forth, saying, "Dear, thou knowest that no mortal power can part my soul from thine!" the man found that they were almost within sight of land. And the Captain said, "Before daybreak to morrow we shall cast anchor, and ere noon shall we be all on shore." Then great joy filled the hearts of that ship's company because of their return, but the man had no part in it, for his soul was sick because of the voices of the sea.

Night drew in on that day with a great darkness, and the stars were hidden from sight, and the man, sitting in his accustomed place, strove eagerly to catch if it were but the echo of a whisper, yet he heard nothing. Fear came on him, lest the voices had departed; great longing grew within him, and he was almost beside himself with pain, when, about the third watch of the night, the mysterious music once more filled his ears, and the fair mist herself at the last became visible to him; and the man seeing the light of her eyes gave up his soul in an ecstasy of wonder, and her kisses lay upon his mouth, and he was utterly possessed of her.

Yet, on the morrow, as his feet touched the land, the man remembered his love; but there was a strangeness in that recollection as of something which he would but could not wholly bring to mind, and he turned himself about, as one but half awake, before he took the pathway by the blue waters which led to the garden, and as he walked under the aloe hedge by which it was defended, he was aware of a fair white canopy fringed with silver, and raised aloft on four crimson standards which showed plain above the thicket of roses wherein he had left his love. And he gazed curiously on the canopy as on something unexpected and unknown, and he made haste to the entrance portals, and passing in, found the little swing gate open, and so, pushing through the roses, came to where this strange thing was. And, having come to the canopy, he saw beneath it a bier covered with violets and asphodel and roses, and anemones of white and scarlet, and beneath the flowers he saw the dead face of the fair woman whom he had loved.

Speaking to those that stood near, the man said, "Who hath done this?" and those who stood near answered, "Our lady sickened and faded not many days after thy departure, and yestereven, about the third watch of the night, she died."

Then the man knew that he had slain his love, and, turning from the bier, he took the pathway by the blue waters, and entering into the black shadow of the pine woods by the rocks he was lost to sight.

The Shrine of Love

A GIRL arose in the morning and threw open those windows of her bed-chamber that looked towards the East, and, as she did so, she beheld her garden, that it was very fair. Now, there were many roses in her garden, and sweet lavender, and white jasmine, and in all the borders thereof were blue violets. And, as she looked on her garden, she saw that all these flowers were in bloom, and she said, "The Spring hath surely passed this way, in the night, while we slept!" But, when she went out into the garden, and saw the footprints of him who had been there, she knew the footprints to be those of Love.

And, when the girl saw how beautiful the feet of Love had made all that place, heaviness came upon her, and sorrow, for she thought, "Had I not been found sleeping, I, too, should have beheld his face!" And, as the days went by, she left off from taking pleasure in her garden, for its beauty was become to her as a reproach, since it seemed that Love must have held her unworthy, else he would have called to her, as he passed her windows.

Being, therefore, sore perplexed, the girl opened the gate of her garden, for she was minded to seek counsel of a wise woman, in whose right hand was the gift of all things, and who dwelt, not far from that place, in the Valley of St. John, hard by the Fountain of Tears.

Now, the Valley of St. John was in a cleft, beneath a high mountain, and the road thither went amongst the rocks, in steep places and difficult, so that the girl was footsore, and very weary, before she came nigh to the dwelling of the woman. And, when she had come nigh she espied her, whom she sought, robed in scarlet and all-glorious with the sun; having, at her back, rocks of black marble and of yellow that were as a throne whereon she sat, and, in her lap, were golden blooms of ever-lasting flowers,—for none but these would grow in that desolate valley. And, the shadows of the mountains, over against her, were lying before her, where the waters of that fountain went past her feet. And the girl entered into the shadows and stood before the woman. And, when she had looked upon her face, she was afraid, for the face of the woman was as a stone, and in her eyes was no pity; yet, taking heart from the strength of that great desire which she had towards Love, the girl knelt before her and told her all the cause of her coming, and how that Love, himself, had visited her garden whilst she slept. Yet, when she had done speaking, the woman kept silence, and, thinking that perchance she heard her not— for the noise of the waters below was very loud in their ears—the girl began again to tell of the coming of Love and of the glory of her garden, and, as she told of these things, she spoke even as one that had been wronged. Then the woman that sat there put forth her hand and stayed her, saying, "What more wouldest thou? Is it not

59

enough?" And, at these words, the girl was abashed before her.

Almost now was she ready to have gone her way, knowing not how she might claim that which she had it in her mind to ask, for the lips of the woman were set and her voice was very bitter, and the girl thought, "Perhaps it is even so, for what am I, that I should have beheld his footprints!" But, as she mused, at the last her tongue was loosed, and she spoke again and said, "Ere I go hence, I pray thee be favourable unto me, and grant me that gift that I shall ask!" And the girl offered the woman all those things that were hers, yea, even the garden that had been made beautiful by the feet of Love. And the woman said, "What is thy desire?" And the girl made answer, "Since I would fain know him whose eyes make all things beautiful, give me a gift, that shall be acceptable unto him, so that I may enter into his temple and look upon his face!"

At this, the woman laughed the girl to scorn, saying, "Thou, even thou, wouldest know Love! Are thine eyes clear enough for the light of his countenance?" And she said, moreover, "Child, show me thy hands." And, when she had looked upon her hands, she said, "Lo! see now thy folly and the vanity of thy desire! Thou wouldest bear a gift to the temple of Love, that thou mayest know the Lord thereof; are these thy hands strong to the bearing of so great a burden?"

But the girl would not be gainsaid, and she answered the wise woman, in these words, "All that I have is thine; grant me only that gift whereby I may enter into the temple of Love." Then the woman, seeing that she might not be denied, arose from the place where she sat, and she took a pitcher of clay that she had by her and filled it at the Fountain of Tears that was near her dwelling. And she gave it to the girl, saying, "Look to it; for thine arms are feeble; yet, if but a drop be spilled by the way, so shalt thou find the doors of the temple shut against thee; neither mayest thou then turn back hither, for thy garden shall be no refuge unto thee." Then the girl went forth from that place, esteeming herself happy in forsaking all those things that had been hers, since she bore in her hands the pitcher of tears, which should be an acceptable gift at the shrine of Love.

Now the road to the temple, wherein was the shrine of Love, lay over the mountains of the East, and the girl knew not the way, nor could she ask counsel of any, seeing that all they whom she met derided her. And she took the dawn for her guide; setting her face, daily, towards the rising of the sun, whilst as yet the dews of the morning were upon the earth. And the labour of the way was great and that burden of tears, which had been given unto her, lay heavy on her hands, and, in her tribulation, her beauty fell away from her, even as a garment that is worn. Then all they that beheld her despised her, and she became as a fool in the eyes of men. And the fires of heaven consumed her flesh by day, and the frosts of the night held her prisoner, and the very winds mocked her, for the times and the seasons were against her. And, when many days and nights were past, and the months drew to years, till the girl knew not the count thereof, it was so, that her heart failed her: and, in her sore trouble and anguish, she heard two voices communing one with another, and one said, "Lo! I lay at ease on my bed, and my beauty was a crown to me, and all men worshipped me, for all the fruits of the earth were mine, and now is there any beggar so miserable that he shall not be preferred before me, if set in comparison with me?" But the other answered and said, "Wouldest thou, indeed, die, not having seen the face of Love? Is there anything in the heaven above, or in the earth beneath, that is like unto him? Yea! even they that go down into the pit praise him!" And, at these words, the girl took up, once more, that her burden of tears, and went her way, but her strength was well nigh gone from her, and she was as one altogether distraught with misery.

And it came to pass, on the evening of the same day, that she entered into a vast plain, but, as she entered into it, the track, which she had followed thither, disappeared, and at every step her feet sank into the deep sands. Then her soul fainted within her, and, in her great weakness, she sank to the ground, giving herself up for lost, and saying, "Surely I am accursed and utterly forsaken; neither, at my dying, shall there be any to pity me!" And, so saying, in her despair, she lifted her eyes to the hills that were on the further side of the plain. As she did so, she saw the purple shadows of the night falling over the hillside, and it was to her as if a shining, even of silver, lay behind the shadows. And her spirit was uplifted at that sight, so that she forgot her weakness, and she arose, and would fain have pressed forward on her way, for she said, "Of a surety, the mystery of days is glorious upon the hillside, and the Lord of that place is Love!" But, on a sudden, the thick darkness of the night compassed her about; so, coming to a little place of grass, near to where she heard water running, she lay her down, if so be that she might rest, but her sleep was troubled, for she dreamed, ever, that the day had dawned, and lo! the sun was up and shone upon the gates of the temple which she sought, but the pitcher, that had been full, was empty. Then, remembering the words of the wise woman in the Valley of St. John, how that she said, "Take heed, for if but a drop be spilled by the way, so shalt thou find the doors of the temple shut against thee!" the girl wept in her sleep, and, so weeping, she awoke. And, when she awoke, she stretched forth her hand and found the pitcher that it was full, and as she touched it, she thought, "Had it been empty, then these eyes had filled it!"

At this, seeing that the morning was at hand, for the blue mists that veiled the wondrous shining on the hillside were touched with light, the girl arose, and having bathed herself in the clear waters of the stream, near which she had slept, she crossed over to the other side, and found there a path, which had before escaped her eyes, leading up into the hills. And, following this path, she came presently to a thicket, the trees whereof were covered with blossoms of scarlet, and everywhere about their trunks were creeping plants, and the giant flowers of these plants were so silver white that they shone like stars in the darkness. And, as the girl entered into the thicket, all that company of birds that were there began to sing, and their song was in praise of the dawn and of Love. And, at the sound of their voices, there was a great murmur and stirring in the thicket, for all things rejoiced thereat, and the furred creatures of the wood came forth in their beauty, and they gambolled before her, and the girl saw them; and the feathered ones also she saw, bright-crested and glorious, for all these knew her to be the servant of Love and shunned her not. On this wise, the loneliness of the way made gladsome by their company, the girl went onwards till, towards the noontide, she came to a fair meadow which was as a garden of flowers, and there were many-coloured butterflies upon the flowers, and beyond that meadow were steps of white marble going up to where was a high terrace, and beyond that terrace was the shining of the temple wherein dwelt the Lord whom she sought.

Then, seeing others standing upon the terrace, the girl went up thither, that she might join herself to their company. And, having come there, she found that they were but in an outer place, and she saw that beneath the terrace, whereon they stood, were the waters of that sacred lake, whereby the temple was encompassed, and, in the midst of the lake, she saw the foundations thereof rising out of the waters, but when she would have looked upon the temple itself she could not, for the radiance of its walls was as of fire. Yet, upon the causeways, leading to the golden gates of the temple, was she able to look, and on the quays of marble which were at the edge of the waters on all sides, and everywhere she saw that place was strewn with pink roses, and with white acacia blooms, and in all the buildings of the outer courts were balconies hung with cloths of silver and of gold, and with wreaths of flowers tied with silken strings of crimson and of azure. And, when the girl had looked on all these things, she beheld herself and knew her own wretchedness, and she saw those that stood near, that their raiment was very beautiful, and how that they bare, in their hands, gifts of all things desirable in the eyes of men. Then her heart failed her, for she thought, "I may not soil with my presence the fair shining of his sanctuary!"

Now, as the sun was full risen, the door keeper, that told the tale of the gifts, which were brought daily by worshippers to that temple, opened wide the doors that were on the terrace, and he came forth, bearing in his hand a silver staff, and bid all those that were waiting there to pass within. But, when he motioned to her to follow, the girl would not, and she humbled herself in her shame, withdrawing herself a little apart, as one fearing to enter, and she bowed herself to the ground, and as she bowed herself, she prayed, saying, "Ah! dear Lord, let me at least die within thy gates!" for, in her abasement, she believed herself no longer worthy to look upon the face of Love.

It happened so, that, in these days, there was grief amongst all them that worshipped at the shrine; in that, the face of their Lord was always veiled; for his temple had, in days gone by, been defiled of the unfaithful, and he, himself, had been driven forth ashamed, and, albeit, that he was now restored to his throne and seat on high among men, yet were the tokens of that defilement visible, and within the sanctuary, where he himself abode, were stains of blood which defaced the whiteness of the pavement beneath his feet; nor could they be made clean by any washing, even of the sacred waters which were round about the shrine. So, day by day, the pavement was strewn with roses, and the worshippers, regarding not the stains thereon, entered freely with their gifts, and heard daily the words of the law of Love, which one read from the book, which was on a table at the entrance. Only the face of Love was always veiled.

And on that day in which the girl stood at the doors of the temple, it came to pass that, when the gifts, which had been brought within, had been taken, he that counted them said, "There is yet one without, and she is ashamed to enter, for she hath naught in her hands save a pitcher of tears." But, as he spake these words, the voice of the Lord was heard, from beneath the veil, saying, "Hath she full measure?" And, they that stood by answered him, saying, "Yea! Oh! Lord. She hath full measure, even to the brim."

Then the word of the Lord went forth and the gates of gold were opened, and the girl, clothed about with misery, and having in her hands the pitcher of tears, was brought within the sanctuary. And Love, himself, arose at her coming and, as she set her feet upon the roses of his shrine, he descended the steps of the throne, and taking from her that pitcher of tears, which she had borne all the days of her youth, he brake it on the pavement beneath his feet. And the waters of affliction flowed out upon the stains thereof, and they were cleansed, insomuch that where had been stains as of blood, the marble was white as snow.

And Love withdrew the veil that had been before his face, so that the girl, after her long tribulation and anguish, beheld the countenance of that merciful one, whose service is peace, and she became glorious in his sight. And when one that stood by said, "Art thou not sore weary of the way, and of thy burden?" she made reply, saying, "Lo! I have no remembrance of those days, save in the gifts of compassion and strength, for have I not now looked upon the face of Love!"

The Outcast Spirit

A GIRL was born of the desire that her father, the son of a great man, had unto a beggar-maid. But, when the great man heard that his son had taken the beggar to wife, he cast him out from his doors, bidding him to live as befitted one that had his liking in those of low estate.

Then the man's soul was heavy and the beggar reproached him, for she had thought to wed her rags with wealth and ease, and her words stung the man like adders' tongues, seeing that he had lost all for her sake, and their days were very sorrowful. So it was that when a child was born to them there was no joy in the man's heart, and the milk of the woman's breasts was bitter.

The gold and silver which the man had brought with him from his father's house were soon spent. Hunger sat with them at meat, nor, when eventide befell, was there any bed for them to lie on. In his sore need the man bethought him of his younger brother, and he went to him and craved a gift at his hands, but his younger brother, being in fear of his father, refused him. Nor was there any help of any other man. And the reviling of the beggar was as a sharp sword, and her curses were like stones.

And things were so, that, as the child grew, she saw the evil things of the world and the hard things thereof, yet was she undefiled: only she became very silent, and her lips were as those of one that is dumb. At the last, it came to pass that the father knew himself to be sick unto death, and seeing the girl, his daughter, to be excellently fair and even as a light shining in the darkness, he sent her to his own people, that they might take her unto them for their name's sake. But they would not, and one refused her, saying, "There are kitchen wenches enough and to spare already within our walls."

When he heard these things, the father was sore grieved, but the beggar laughed, for she had it in her mind how she would make money of her daughter.

Not many days after, seeing that the man could not move, but lay as one that was dead, the beggar spoke aloud of the bargain she had made and counted the pieces of money before his face, and the girl, sitting there, watched her the while with a great terror in her eyes. And, in her rejoicing, the woman arose, and coming near to the place where he, who had been son to the great man, now lay low, she chinked the money in her hands, crying, "This, truly, is more than ever I thought to have gotten by thee!"

But, as she spoke these words, he, who lay there before her, raised himself, as by a great effort, and caught her by the hair, drawing her down backwards upon his knees, and all the money which she had in her hands was scattered on the floor. When he now had her at his mercy, the man so twisted the kerchief that was about her neck that in a short space she died, making no moan. Having done this, he turned, and seeing the girl, his daughter, watching him, he pointed to the door, crying "Go! This is the house of Death."

Then the girl fled out into the streets, and he who had bargained for her coming there shortly after, found her not. And, when this one saw the pieces of money that the beggar had received of him, scattered on the floor, and, looking to the bed, beheld the body of the man fallen forward upon that of the woman his wife, he was afraid. So he went his way, and the people of the house entered in and took up the money, and, sending for a priest, they paid therewith for the burial of those two;— the son of the great man and the beggar his wife. But no one took any thought for the girl.

Now, when she had gone forth in her fear, the girl would fain have taken refuge with her mother's kinsfolk, and for that night, only they gave her shelter, but on the morrow, seeing that her ways were strange to them, they hardened their hearts and drave her from their doors, saying, "Go hence, we are poorer than thou!" Then these words were in her ears, even as the echo of her father's voice crying "Go!" And again she went forth and walked in the streets and ways. But, as the second night drew on, she was much troubled, for she knew not where she was, nor whether there were any of whom she might ask a lodging.

And as she came out from a narrow lane leading down a steep place on the outskirts of the city, she heard, beneath her feet, the sound of rushing waters, and knew that she was standing on the bridge where a great river from the snow mountains passed on its way to the sea. The waters called to her, and she followed them until she came to a causeway not far from the shore, and on each side it was defended against the drifting sands by a low wall. The night was very still, and in the darkness she heard voices singing and, as the waves rolled in, the voices rose higher, and this was what they sang in her ears:

"Three men stood on the quarter-deck,
One had a red ring round his neck,
And two the salt seas could not drown
For the sin that was sinned in their father's town.

Three women met in the garden patch,
One had lifted the hangman's latch,
Two, they carried the nameless thing
The witch fiend's daughter had bade them bring.

When six shall meet on the whirlpool's brink,
The souls of seven shall with them sink,
And the folk of hell shall frighted flee
Before the face of that company."

When the girl heard these words she was afraid, and would have gone further, but coming to an opening in the wall she espied some stairs, and at the foot of the stairs was light, as of a fire. So, being very cold, she went down them, and there, by a stage at the water's edge to which many boats were moored, she found a great company of boatmen, and by the stage there was a fire, and those

71

boatmen whose voices she had heard singing in the darkness were sitting round it. Going up to them, the girl then asked of them that she might warm her hands at their fire, for it was winter and the cold was very bitter. Then they said, "Draw near," and she drew near. But, when she stood in the light of the fire and they saw her, one knew her for the daughter of that beggar who had wedded with the son of the great man, and he derided her, saying, "Where be thy serving-men, thy runners and thy women? Lo! this is but poor state for the lord thy father's daughter!" And, when the girl answered him not, he swore that she should sing to him, saying, " Come, let us hear thy voice!" and taking her by the shoulders, would have forced her to sit down with him.

At this moment, on a sudden, there were lights on the stair, and the priest, who had come from the burying of her dead, stepped down to the stage that he might be put across the bay. Seeing the girl standing there, he called her to him and sharply questioned her with many questions, but she could give no account of herself, nor of how she had come to that place.

At this the priest was angered, and he bade her forthwith confess how it had come to pass that she had left the dead, saying that it should go ill with her if she concealed aught from him. Then the girl, who had eaten nothing since that hour, remembering all the terror of it, became as one distraught, and stretching forth her hands before her, "Go!" she cried, and fell down at his feet as one dead. At this the priest, thinking much evil of her, for he had heard of the money that had been found on the floor and that the death of the beggar had seemed strange to all men, was sore perplexed, asking himself what he should do.

Had it not been for shame of those that stood by, he would have left her, but, having spoken as one that was in authority over her, this misliked him. And he thought, "Should I take her to a religious house, they would not willingly receive her, seeing that she hath no dowry!" but, at the last, he said to the boatmen, "Take up the girl and put her in the boat, and steer the boat for the water-gate of the palace that is on the other side." And they did so.

Now when they had come to the stairs of the palace, the priest bade them that were with him to take the girl and carry her into the hall where the great man, her father's father, sat at meat. And when they were come there, the priest stayed his steps on the threshold, and so standing he spoke with a loud voice and said, " Lo! my Lord, thy son whom thou hadst cast out is dead, and the beggar whom he had taken to wife is dead also, and this, his child, have I brought unto thee that thou mayest give order concerning her."

And the great man answered the priest never a word, but he called his servants, and bid them that they should give him to eat.

As for the girl, whether it were for pity or for shame, he desired the women that were there in the hall to take her and carry her to a far chamber. And when she was come to herself, they put black garments upon her, and they gave her counsel that by no means should she show herself, in that palace, where she might offend the eyes of her father's father or of any of her kindred.

So the girl lived her life alone, and no man cared for her. By day, she sat solitary, and when the evening drew on and the night was at hand she walked in a fair garden that was beneath her windows, and in the garden was a terrace, raised between two rows of cypress, upon the wall over above the sea, and at times, looking thence, beyond the purple shadows of the twilight, she could see the eternal snows on distant mountains flushing scarlet against the sunset sky.

It came to pass that one night, when she was walking in that garden, the girl met Death, and he seemed to her not terrible, but only very sad, and she went near to him and said, "I, too, am sad, and my heart is heavy; let me be of thy company!" And, she put her hand in his.

Then Death held up her fingers to the light and said, "There should be many days 'twixt me and thee," and he refused her. And, as she turned from him, she heard from below the voices of men singing in a boat close under the wall whereon the terrace was raised, and these were the words which came to her ears:

> "And two the salt seas would not drown
> For the sin that was sinned in their father's town."

Then, she knew that the song which they sang was even the same as that she had heard in the darkness on the night when the priest, who had buried her dead, had met her by the water's edge, and had brought her to the palace of her father's father.

Seeing now that she had no place on earth and that Death would not willingly have her of his company, the girl sought for herself the means whereby she might part from life. And, before many days had gone by, they that entered her chamber in the morning found her on her bed, and when they spoke she answered not, neither did she stir when they laid hands upon her. Then one of the women took a mirror and held it before her mouth, and, seeing that the silver remained without stain, they said, "She is dead." So, they went and told the old man, her father's father, and he said, "It is well." And, having sewn her decently in a white shroud, they laid lilies on her and shining daisies from the garden in which she had walked, and they carried her forth and buried her.

Now, the girl had thought that her spirit, in the hour of her parting, should escape and should wander, free from fear, in the palace that had been her father's habitation. But it was otherwise. For, even as she passed, the spirits of the house came about her, and they were a vast company, crying, "Who art thou? How camest thou hither?" So, they drave her before them, and, as she fled from room to room of that palace, they gathered to an innumerable host. Then she went forth into the garden and stayed her flight at the terrace walk where she had met Death, but even there she was pursued by that terrible company.

At this, the spirit knew that for those who have no place in life, neither is there any place in death, and shuddering, passed out upon the night.

Heart's Desire

CROWNING a place of rocks, that rises high above the sea coast with its front towards the morning sun, there stood, in past times, an ancient city close imprisoned within its walls. And they that lived there had so built that place—fearing lest their neighbours, who were mighty in war, should fall upon them unawares—that no man could enter into their streets save by one of two gates,—the gates of the East and of the West; and, at each of these gates were square towers of great height and strength, whence they that kept watch could securely behold that vast country which lay beneath them on each side. So all they in the city dwelt in peace, for by sea might no man come at them, seeing that the currents of those waters were most treacherous, neither on the landward side was there any safe means of approach, for, on the north, there was a steep precipice which rose so high above the lands below that often if one, who had his habitation on the walls, looked forth, he saw naught but the clouds of heaven flying beneath him, even as it were birds on the wing.

Now, within that city not far from the Gate of the West, was a house unlike to any of the others that were in those streets. It was more ancient than any and fairer far, in the fashion of its building, than those that were its neighbours. And that house, which was of many storeys, bore name "The House of Whiteness," for they that had so builded it had made to each storey a facing of white marble sculptured with marvellous fine work, insomuch that men wondered to look upon it, nor might any, at that time, do the like. Nor was it known by whom the house had been so builded, nor on what account, neither was the curse by which its hearth lay desolate manifest to any, only a deep silence lay behind the closed doors and windows, and none could say that he had been within and learned the secret of that silence.

And, it came to pass, in the early dawn of a winter's day, that he who watched at the Gate of the West, look-ing out above the morning mists, as they rolled slowly away from the rocks below him, knew that there were travellers on the road. Nor, at the first, was it plain to him what these might be, for he saw them dimly, but as shapes moving within the shroud of floating vapour that hung about them; but presently, as they drew nearer the eyes of the watcher discerned that they were all aged men, and, as he looked he bethought him of those four carven in marble, that looked forth from above the doors of "The House of Whiteness." For above those doors were the figures of four waiting, in whose hands were great gifts, even Death and Life, the Sun and all the Stars of Heaven. And the watcher remembered that which was lettered on the scroll that was graven beneath those figures, for the letters thereof were:

Nor Death, nor Life, nor Snow, nor Fire,
Shall stay the foot of Heart's Desire.

And, the watcher thinking on these things, and looking upon those that had now drawn near, knew them to be the Lords of the House of Whiteness, and he made haste and called to him that kept the Gate of the West, saying, "Open! For the Lords of the House of Whiteness be upon the road." So he that kept the gate opened to them, and they that were upon the road entered within the city and betook them to that their house which stood not far from the gate.

Now, when the sun was fully up, all the men of that city went each one to his work and to his labour till the evening, for their Prince was no easy taskmaster that they should lightly disobey him, and the women and girls also were set to their daily toil; only the young children made glad after their fashion, playing, as it pleased them, in the streets or on the ramparts. And, of these, a certain band, according to their wont, made haste that they might be the first to reach that little open space, near to the Gate of the West, in which was the House of Whiteness. And even as these little ones came from their doors into the main street of the town, they saw, floating in the sky, far above the roofs of the houses, a silken banner of many colours, and they knew that the banner hung from the scarlet standard, which was set up before the entrance to that house. And, every child that looked upon the banner, as it waved in the air, saw his or her favourite colour brightening and trembling in the morning light. And the children, seeing this, grew wild with pleasure, for, within the folds of the banner, each one read the promise of his heart's desire, and they clapped their hands and shouted for joy. Then, as if moved by one consent, they ran madly through the streets till they came before the old house. And when they had come there, they were astonished, for there was no change in it such as they had thought to find. The shutters were, indeed, gone from the windows, and the door—which had been ever closed——now stood wide, but this only made that place look the more desolate. The marble steps of the entrance were unswept, they were covered with filth and refuse; broken cobwebs fell torn and ragged from every opening; the window-panes were thick with the dust of years; the wood-work of the frames was rotten, even the flooring, which showed through the open doorway, was full of treacherous holes. What secrets might lie within the yawning darkness of those doors, none could guess! Yet after a while, looking closely, it seemed to the children that there were certain shapes dimly to be seen, the shapes of aged men, in dark clothing, standing silent on each side, behind an empty counter.

Now, when the children beheld these things they were checked in their joy, and all that little crowd stood still, abashed and amazed at the strange deception, but, at the last, one, the boldest of them, for he was the son of wealthy parents, holding his money tight within his hand, stepped across the gloomy threshold, and the others followed slowly behind him. But, the old gray-bearded men spoke not, neither did they move, and their eyes were as if they saw not those eager frightened faces that were uplifted to them. At this the boy, half angry, rapped with his money on the counter and said in a clear voice, "See, Sirs, whoever you may be, here I have money, take what you will, only give me my heart's desire!" And, the old men answered, all speaking as one, "Today we have it not. Lo! the sun shines and the stars rise for all; tomorrow, perchance, it shall be given unto you." At this, all the children crept away, murmuring, yet half ashamed.

But, on the morrow, and for many days after, with the early dawn they saw that banner floating on high, and as each little one beheld, in its shining folds, the colour that he loved, he was seized again with the same delight that carried his feet, in spite of repeated failure, to seek, within the doors of the House of Whiteness, that which was ever promised only for the morrow. But, none the less, did the children grow weary of waiting. Some even began to think themselves befooled and would go no longer to the old house, though they still would hoard, for the morrow that came not, all such monies as were given to them by their mothers to their spending, and would ask each day of those that did their errand, "Tell us, we pray you, what news?"

For many weeks the boy, who had been the first to enter within those doors, continued to put his patient question every morning, and when the others chid him and asked him why he would be thus deceived of those

that were Lords of that House, he would answer, steadfastly, "They deceive us not. Surely, on the morrow, shall
they that are faithful receive each one his heart's desire!"
Yet, at the last, he, too, lost courage and left off from
hope. Nor did he slip away, secretly, as some had done,
but when, after many days, he heard those aged ones re-
peat again with one accord the tardy promise of "Tomorrow," he turned and looked them in the face, crying,
"No! No! Today for me. Today or never. There are other
houses in this town where I can buy for my money much
that is fair in my eyes! How know I, indeed, whether
there be any such one and only good as my heart de-
sireth? How know I if there be any tomorrow?" To this
the old men that were Lords of the House of Whiteness
made no answer, and so the boy went from them.

He went from them, and many there were that went
with him, all such, they said, as were not fools, nor was
it long before the boy and those his companions began
to make mock of all they who still were faithful—setting
out on that fruitless errand with every dawn. One by one
the children now dropped away till at last there was never a crowd in the old street; they dropped away till, of all
they that had greeted the shining banner in their morning gladness, a girl-child only remained. And, seeing her
to be very frail and sad, all those others were used to
come about her with jeers and with laughter, so that she
went forth on her way in terror. And, some upbraided
her with her folly, and others said, "Nay, she is but idle,
and to gossip in the House of Whiteness is her pastime!"
Had, however, any of these that so rebuked her, followed her within those doors to which she daily had resort

they would have heard no words save that prayer which was ever on her lips, "See, Sirs, here is all that I have! Take it and give unto me that good which is my heart's desire! " And, to this, they that were there returned her ever the self-same answer, "It is so, this day, that we have it not. Perchance, on the morrow, it shall be given unto thee!" And with this hope she needs must be content, yet in her soul there was a great sadness that grew deeper with each succeeding dawn.

In the end, it pleased all the children of that town to meet the little one at her door every morning with angry cries and threats, and so they hunted her all her way, hanging round the steps by which she entered, and greeting her when she came out thence with loud shouts and much bitter jesting. So day by day the child went in the greater fear of them, and day by day her prayer grew fainter on her lips, and her soul was sick within her so that hardly might she dare lift her unhappy eyes to the inscrutable faces of those old men, that were the Lords of the House of Whiteness.

The summer came, and with the waxing glory of the sunlit days the sorrows of the child increased. One morning she rose very weary after a night of dreams, and looking forth at the hour of her out going, she trembled, for all they that of old had been her playmates, and her companions were watching for her by the gate, and at this time their hearts were hardened against her. And, when they saw her, they cried, "Out upon thee, thou fool! There shall none such be of our company. Cease then this thy folly that plagueth us, or we will cast thee out." And, so saying, they made them ready with

sticks and with stones to drive her from that town. And
they that were of her own house were against her; yea,
even her own mother reviled her, insomuch that her
heart failed her, and she said, "Let me not live alone! Oh!
my brothers, my sisters! I will cease it." And she returned
within her doors, and they left her.

And, when the echoes of their footsteps died away,
a great anguish fell upon the child, but, as she lifted her
eyes to the banner, where it hung listlessly in the burning sky, she saw, shining through her tears, those colours
which she had loved. And her fear fell away from her at
this sight, and she set forth once more on her way to the
House of Whiteness. At the first, too, she went forward
boldly as one that walked in his right, for in her heart was
a new courage, and, since it was by then mid-day, there
were none to stay her in the streets. Before long, however, it was as if she heard a footfall near her, and there-
upon she was possessed of fright and ran as if all they
that had mocked her had been at her heels pursuing. So
she came to that little place that was before the house she
sought, and, when she had come there, she feared lest
the doors should be already closed, for it was later than
her wont, and behold, two of those grey-bearded ones
that were Lords of the House were, indeed, already on
the threshold bearing between them the shutters wherewith to close the windows thereof. But, when they saw
her running and looked upon her outstretched hands,
and knew her to be offering to them, yet again that single coin, which was all that she had, they drew to either
side of the steps and stood still awaiting her, and she
coming up passed within the doors, and they followed

her. Within the doors all was as it had ever been; out of the same dark fathomless emptiness shone the steadfast, silent, aged faces! "Will they then," she thought in her despair, "never grant to my beseeching any other word than 'Tomorrow'!" And she thought also, so weary was she, "Tomorrow may come too late for such a one as I!" Nevertheless, she held out that her money and entreated them yet again, saying, "Here, Sirs, is money. Take it, only fulfil the promise unto me. Grant me, I pray you, that one good thing that is my heart's desire!"

Then, the old men, even they that were Lords of the House of Whiteness, answered her with one voice, "Be it unto thee according to thy prayer." And they gave to her her heart's desire. And, they said, moreover, "Be secret. So shall none know that which thou hast to thy reward, for, shouldest thou betray us, it shall go hardly with thee!" And, when the child had received of them her heart's desire, they took from her that coin, which was even all that she had, and that House was again closed.

But the children, even all they that had been her companions and her playmates, as they knew not of her fortune, so they still despised her, and many rebuked her, and to others she was as one they knew not, yet she alone had obtained that which all desired to possess.

The Hangman's Daughter

A T that time the kingdom of France was divided against itself, and the princes and chiefs of the people fought against the King and against his princes; and there was heavy trouble throughout the land. For all men went forth to war, insomuch that the husbandman forgot to gather his harvest, and in the springtime there was none to sow the seed. Yet there were not wanting many that came to their advantage thereby, making profit out of those things by which others were brought to their destruction.

And word came of the war, and of the chances thereof, to one that dwelt alone with his mother in a strong castle of the hill country in the East. And this man bore a great name that was shamed by his poverty, and upon the mother there lay the burden of a long sorrow, for her lord had been brought back to her dead in the day that her son was born. And the enemies of that race, seeing them to be, in those years, without defence, had stripped the woman and her child of all their possessions, so that when the boy was come to age, in all that country, which he had been heir to, no man called him master or lord.

Moreover, those others would have taken from him even the castle wherein he dwelt, but it so happened that, at what time they would have seized on it, they were uneasy amongst themselves, and, the war breaking forth soon after, they drew away in their strength to the West, where was the chief of the fighting, saying, "Let this place be till we come again."

Yet, for all that they made so sure, many months passed and they returned not, and it seemed to all men that the troubles in the land should have no end, for none could tell whether the King, or they that were the enemies of his house, should have the mastery. At the first, in truth, they of the people had the advantage, but the King's counsellors were crafty, and when they saw that men were grown weary of the strife, they cried, "Peace!" saying, "The soul of the King longeth for peace!" But when they had brought the chiefs of the people to treat of times and of conditions, they broke off that treaty, now on one pretence, now on another, seeking how they might divide their foes amongst themselves. And, on a day when things were at such a pause, it came to pass even as those of whom the King took counsel would have had it. For the princes and chiefs of the people, putting faith in the words of the King, fought against each other, counting the spoils of victory as already won. Then they that were with the King, seeing in these divisions their looked-for opportunity, made haste and came up with the hosts of the people very swiftly, while their chiefs were in the heat of that disorder, and the King's generals posted his forces in such wise that those rebellious ones might not refuse to do them battle; and there was a set battle, in the which many of the chiefs of the people were slain, and all those that were with them were put to flight. And the armies of the King pursued them, and of those that fled, all such as fell into the hands of their pursuers were put to the sword.

But a remnant escaped from the slaughter. And these were in no wise willing to submit themselves unto the mercy of the King; so they betook them to a walled city by the sea, and made haste to garnish it and furnish it before their enemies should be come at them! And the hosts of the King drew thither, and the strong place, which that rebellious people had thought should be to them a tower of defence, became as a snare in which they were taken, they and all those that were with them. And the hand of the King was heavy upon them in his wrath, and he, thinking himself sure of his prey, laid a siege before the city and set watch on all sides, so that they that were within might not issue forth, neither might any man carry them succour from without. And the captains of the King set their pavilions on the high ground near the coast, and the whole land was overspread with their hosts. For, being as at that time drawn into winter quarters, much people had joined themselves to them, and the camp was become like unto a great city, so vast was the throng of those that pressed within or hung upon the outskirts thereof. Theft, murder, and violence were in all the byways. Now, the man knew naught of these things when he entreated his mother that she should let him go.

And he thought to find the armies over against each other in the open field, and he schemed in his mind how he should come at the King, hoping that by some action of credit he might take fortune captive and restore the honour of his house. But his mother was loth that he should approach the King as one disguised; for their estate was fallen so low, that of all those gentlemen to whom they were allied there was not one to whom she dared address him; and though her son was as a giant for strength and stature, yet was he all unskilled in knightly exercises. But he prevailed with her that she should let him go. And in the hour of their parting her heart was very sorrowful, for he was dear unto her, not only in that he was her son, but for those virtues in his nature which were clouded by their misfortune. And she placed about his neck a golden medal, with a chain of pearls, and she charged him straitly that he should bring it her again, for that it had been a gift given her of his father; and she commended him to the saints, and she blessed him, saying, "May the Lord be with thee, in all thy ways that thou goest!" and so he departed from her.

Now, he went forth from his gates alone, having none to bear him company, for of all the servants of the lord his father there remained faithful only such as were well stricken in years. And, as he descended the steep ways which led down from the castle into the plain beneath, there went at his heels the evil fates that dogged him, and his soul was filled with bitterness; for, looking out above the mists of the dawn, he beheld the sun coming across the far off hills, and his rays touched the circles of the river which watered all those lands which should have been his, and made all that water which surrounded the hill on which the castle stood to glisten as it were molten silver. And he turned himself about, and cursed them that had despoiled him; but his mother, watching him as he went, thought that he bade her once more "Farewell," and she blessed him in her heart, praying for that his coming again.

And as he rode in the plain, when it was about his sixth day's journey, the man saw before him one that bore a scarlet pennon worked in gold, and, in a little while, he came up with certain horsemen, who had been sent forth by a great prince of the King's party to bring in recruits for that troop which he had raised, on the borders of the South, at the beginning of troubles. And though his numbers were now full, he that was their leader, looking on the armour of the man,—for he wore his father's armour, black inlaid with silver after the Italian fashion,— saw him to be of no ordinary sort. So he made offers to him, and the man joined himself to them. But on the morrow, as they went on their way, certain merchants whom they met, talked with them, saying, "The King has utterly discomfited them that were in arms against him, and against his authority. He has broken the strength of all that people, and his armies are now camped about their city of refuge." And they said further, "In a little while the war shall be at an end." And the man hearing these things was very sorry, for he thought, "If this is so, how shall I prove myself in the day of battle, or come to the right hand of the King! They that are against me are too strong for me. Before ever I saw the light, judgment was delivered into the hand of mine enemies!" And he would fain have returned by the way that he came, only his word held him.

And, seeing him to be thus heavy in mind, those that rode with him would have mocked him, for they liked him not; his tongue was strange to them, neither were his ways as their ways; but they kept silence before him, being in fear of his great stature and strength. And their leader himself was troubled, for when he had asked of the man his name, he had denied him, saying, "What is that to thee! Call me even as thou listest." And, again, to them that had bidden him declare the place of his birth, he had made answer on the same fashion, for, in his pride of race, he took it amiss that any should seek to know that which he was minded to conceal. And, when he knew those that were his comrades, he despised them, and repented him of his act, for whereas he had reckoned to find amongst them some who, like himself, sought but the occasion whereby they might rise to honour, and would willingly have been instructed by their better experience in all the graver arts of war, he found their talk to be ever of drink, or of dicing, or of such other licence as commonly makes suit to a soldier's life. And, from all these things, the heaviness of his thoughts—keeping pace with the sullenness of his temper—held him aloof.

Yet, when, after many weeks, they were come to the camp, he was curious to see the sights thereof, and when he had stabled his horse and taken up his allotted quarters, he made to go forth alone into the lines. Then, some others of that his troop, seeing him to be but freshly come amongst them, offered him civility, saying, "Be one of us. Let us sup together, and when we have well eaten and drunken, let us go see the women by the walls."

For it was so that the garrison of that rebellious city, being now in sore straits, had driven out from their gates all such as were a burden to them: the old, the sick, and all women and young children. And they had sent out with them a flag of truce, and they had entreated the King that he should give to these a free passage; but he would not, neither would they that were in the city receive them again. Therefore, these wretched ones went in peril of life daily, and they sought for themselves roots of herbs and of grass in the ground below the walls, if so be that by these means they might stay their hunger; but nevertheless many died of famine. And so great was their distress that a woman would sell herself for a crust. And many did so, having no other way whereby they might give to eat to the children and the aged that were with them.

Now, at the first, the man was minded to refuse those that would have had him go with them: they, however, pressed him so that he consented and went. But even as they were on their way to the tavern, where they should drink together, they were aware of a great crowd moving towards the sea, and the man questioned his comrades what it might be. And they made answer lightly, "Surely it is one that shall be hanged." For in each quarter of the camp were gallows standing, and in that quarter, where he that was their prince had his positions, seven such had been set up on a scaffold by the sea, near to a high place, called St. Catharine's Hill. And that spot was accounted a place accurst, and all things evil had their resort thereto. For, by day, the hangman and his brood bought and sold at the gallows' foot, and, at nightfall, men said all the unburied dead were servants unto them. For the bodies of such as had suffered death there were cast into the waters beyond the sands.

When the man, and they that were with him, had come up with the crowd, they pushed on until they had made their way into the midst, and, not far from the scaffold, they saw a youth that was delivered to the executioner, and hard by there was a monk preaching, and at his right a fair woman standing. And the woman was clad all in grey, and her habit, in part, was like to the habit of a nun, but her garments were torn and sullied as with blood. And, as the hangman knotted the rope in his hands, the monk reviled the youth, saying, "Thou fool! Could none other save this holy virgin serve thy turn?" This, he said, knowing her to be one who had followed the prince, who was chief amongst the King's generals, from that religious house wherein they had had their quarters before the great battle. And, for a while, that false virgin had been dear to the prince, but she was now abandoned of her lover, though as yet men knew it not, else had not that youth paid so dearly for his folly. She, the while, looking upon the soldiers that had come up with them, marked the stature and great strength of the man that was newly come into the camp, and seeing the beauty of his arms, and the chain of pearls shining within the collar of his doublet, took him to be some great lord. So, she made signs to him, privily, that he should speak with her; but, even as he would have done so, one that wore a scarlet hood came from among the crowd and whispered her. Then the nun turned herself about quickly, and that other kissed her on the mouth and drew her away. And all those people that were there were astonished, and said, "How is this? She, that was servant to the Lord, hath kissed the hangman's daughter on the mouth." Now, many days passed, and it so fell out that the man saw not these women again.

And the man's heart was very heavy; for though he had come to a place of arms, yet all men lay secure, and they that feasted and made merry were more in number than they that took counsel together. And, when he looked for those hazards, by the which he had accounted himself certain to rise to honour, he heard but of parleys, and marchings, and counter-marchings, and of prisoners taken, not by warlike enterprise, but overmastered by sleight and cunning. For, not many days after his coming, certain of the rebels, in an outer fort, were surprised and slain, what time they had thought themselves secure in the word of accord pledged to them by the King. And the man knew himself to have been deceived when he had thought, by taking service with that army, to draw his house from the obscurity into which it had fallen. And the remembrance of his hopes was bitter unto him. So, it came to pass that when he was mustered, with the others, for any great show, he was slow to be ready; thinking shame that he who would have been a soldier should be called to make sport for women and their gallants.

For, ofttimes, the ladies of the Court, in great splendour, would visit the camp, coming as to any strange sight, and would spend many days with the princes, their kinsmen and lovers, that were with the King. And, at their coming, these would entertain them with tiltings and with banquetings, for there was no lack or stint of aught in the camp, and great provision of all goodly things was brought daily within the lines.

And on a certain day, when the spring drew near, there was much merriment in that troop, for tidings were brought to the camp of the coming of the Queen, and in her train were many ladies, and, amongst them, a passing fair woman to whom he, that was captain over them, was servant. So he bade his men to make them ready, that they might not be behind any that were there in show of reverence. And, that they might be the more magnificent, he promised money, to every man five pieces, saying, "Look to it, that there be none more bravely furnished than they that ride with me!" And he gave them scarves, moreover, of azure and of silver, that were the colours of that lady, that they might wear them in her honour. To every man in his troop he gave a scarf.

And the man was angered at all these things, and in his sullen fit he withdrew himself from the company of his fellows, and went forth on foot, to St. Catharine's Hill, that he might be alone. And, as he came near to that place, one, that espied him, gave warning of his coming. But the man knew it not, and, in a short space, having climbed to the seaward side, he cast himself down upon the grass. And, as he lay there, he looked out over the sea and searched the walls of that city with his eyes, and he beheld those strange shapes crawling beneath the ramparts, that were even as a mass of foulness, in the which no man should know his brother. And, as the man marked these things, he heard sounds of revelry and of laughter passing on the wind, that set that way from the camp. And he turned him and beheld the tents pitched and all that array of martial magnificence, and, on a little point below, he saw the white plume of the King, and behind the King were his generals and that great prince of the church who was his chief minister. At this sight, that nobleness, which remained yet in the man's soul, was troubled, and it seemed to him a small thing, and a contemptible, in a King, having so great force of armed men to do his bidding, that he should ride forth daily, as it were a pastime, to watch, from a safe place, the agony of his people, dying of pestilence and famine.

Now, as he thought on these things, it seemed to the man that he heard the voices of two talking together very closely, and it seemed, also, that these sounds came from that side of the hill which faced towards the south, where was that waste place in which the gallows had been set up. But he gave no heed to the voices, and so heavy was he, with the discontent that oppressed him, that his ears were as closed to the footsteps which then came near by the way of approach behind him. On a sudden, however, one spoke, close at hand, very clear and sweet, saying, "Come!" And, at that call, the man turned himself about, and, at first, he saw naught but the great glory of the sun dropping below St. Catharine's Hill and the fire of his rays which dyed all the rocks with scarlet; but presently, in the heart of the fire, he was aware of one standing, whose garments were crimson as with blood. Even as he looked she passed before him, and, in her passing, she beckoned plainly unto him that he should follow her. And he arose, and followed her, but he could not overtake her. And it was now twilight.

Then the man, having come to a hollow which was in the side of the hill and seeing two ways going from that place, stayed his steps and looked about him that he might, peradventure, discover whither she had gone that led him, but she was beyond his sight, for the sea fog, crawling slowly over the sands, had drawn round all the base of the hill. And, as the man doubted within himself whether he should go further, or not, he heard a soft breathing on his right, and stretching out his hand, thinking to lay hold of that one, whom he had followed, he drew to himself that other, she of the gray habit, whom he first had looked upon at the scaffold foot that day when he had come into the camp. And she put her arms about him and drew him down with her to the grass, saying, "I am weary, rest with me awhile." And the man consented to her. And, when the man left that place, those evil things that were against him had drawn nigh unto him, and that chain, which had been given him of his mother, was no longer about his neck.

On the morrow, when he that commanded the troop gave his orders, he bade every man put himself in readiness, for that the Queen, with her train, was now come very near, and should, most surely, be in the camp before nightfall. And he paid to every man those monies which he had promised, and when all these had seen that their harness was in readiness, and that naught was wanting wherewith they should ride, looking on the gold that was in their hands, they betook themselves, in parties, to the wine-shops. And the man joined himself to a party whereof the chief was one who privily hated him, in that before his coming he had been counted the strongest amongst them, and now feared lest he should have found his master. This one was minded, therefore, if by any means he could compass it, to drive the man forth from that troop.

And, when they had all well drunken, they sat them down to the dice till supper should be come; nor was it long before the man had parted with every piece that he had to him that was his enemy and to those that were in accord with him,—for he was careless of such things, and they were more cunning than he. And, when they saw that his pockets were empty, his comrades mocked him, saying, "Go now to thy lodging, lest worse befall thee, for he that is over us loves not beggars in his troop." But the man was now mad with anger, so that they took him the more easily in their snares that they had set for him, and at the last he staked, on a single throw, all that he had remaining—his arms, his horse, and all those things wherewithal he had made ready to ride on the morrow. Having lost these, too late, he knew himself to be abused, and growing desperate, he waxed wroth, and would have had his adversary by the throat. Then one of those others that were there pushed the bench whereon he sat from beneath him, so that he fell to the ground, and, before ever he could rise, they were all upon him, and overpowered him, and thrust him to the door, crying, "Thou art no longer of our company. Go! sup with the hangman's daughter! And they thrust him out.

And, in his wrath, the man did even as they had said, for he went down towards the sea, and, walking by the sands, came to that place apart and walled against the waters, whereon the gallows had been set up by order of the marshal of the camp. And, coming to that place, he was aware of three shapes that sat there. And the first shape was as that of a man robed in black; and the second he saw to have a gray habit, in part like to the habit of a nun, and the cloak of the third was scarlet, so that the man knew these three to be those whom he had seen at that his first coming to the camp. And the three called to him, as he went by, saying, "Come up hither, and eat with us!" for they knew he was an hungered. And when he had come up to them he of the black robes said, "Lo! wine is a good thing! " And she of the gray habit made answer, "Flesh is better!" And the third, that was younger than they two, and whose face was very fair, even as the face of a young child, replied, "Oh! father, flesh is good and wine is good, but blood is better!" And as she said these things she lifted the cup that was in her hands, and smiled on the man so that he sat down and became one of their company. And, in the soreness of his heart, he told them all that had befallen him, and he joined hands with them, that they should deliver him from his enemy. And, when that supper had an end, the man would fain have left them, but she that had the face of a girl held him, saying, "Pledge me once in the wine-cup before thou goest;" so for the second time he obeyed her, and he pledged her. And the red wine of her cup was as fire on his lips, and he made as if he would have kissed her, but she put him from her, saying, "Nay, but first thou shalt give me a token." And she constrained him.

Then the man bethought him that he had naught that he could give her, save that blessed medal of gold, now made fast within his doublet, the which his mother had placed about his neck at the time of his setting forth on his way to the army of the King. And he was loth to give this unto her. Yet he gave it; and, when she had it in her hands, she drew, from between her breasts, a fine scarlet thread, and by this thread she fastened the medal close about her throat. So the man, having parted with this sacred sign, delivered himself to evil. And he took, for his gift, the kisses of the lips that were red with blood, and, even as he kissed them, a deep slumber fell upon him.

Now, towards the dawning, the man awoke from his sleep, for he was very cold; and he moved himself, and, as he moved, he put his hand on one that lay beside him, and he remembered her whom he had kissed, and thought to have embraced her, but, in the moment that he would have done so, he drew back, for he knew that he had set his mouth to the mouth of one already dead. At this, he was amazed, and, looking more nearly on the face of his neighbour, he beheld the face of him who had robbed him, and mocked him, and had driven him forth from among that company. And, as he looked on this man who had been his comrade, he bethought him of the wine shop and of all that quarrel that befell, and, so thinking, he remembered him of his loss, and cast about in his mind how he should ride that day, seeing that he had lost all his furnishing. Even as he called to mind these things, the blast of a trumpet came shrilly from the camp, and he knew that the dawn had risen, and that the call was to arms. And he looked for those others that should have been there, but he saw no man, for the mists of the morning were even as a shroud lying on all that place, and he rose to his feet and stripped the man that was before him, and so he had his own arms again, and also that scarf that had been his. And, as he did this, he saw, on the throat of the dead, a mark as of a fine thread, and it was like unto thread of scarlet, and he called to mind those silken threads which the hang man's daughter had drawn out, where her garments parted above her breasts. And, as he continued looking, he heard a sound as of sighing, and a voice of weeping came near, saying, "Take him up and throw him over; throw him over, I beseech thee, for if he be found here, I know not what thing they two shall do unto me!" And the man was troubled, for the voice seemed to him as the voice of her whom he had kissed on the mouth, and he called to her, but she came not nigh him, nor could he see aught save the shape of the gallows above his head, but the sighing of the voice was so sore, that, without more ado, he took up the body of him by whom he had been wronged, and cast it over the wall, and the sea received it.

Having done this, he set forth on his way towards the camp, and entering into that stable where the horses of his troop were stalled, found his own standing at the side of that one which had been that of his adversary, and they were both ready saddled and bridled. And, though he doubted somewhat, whether he should or not, he took that which had belonged to the dead, seeing it to be very strong and powerful, and he mounted it and, riding swiftly, overtook the others, his comrades, when as yet they had gone but a little way.

And, when he had come up with them, they looked strangely on him, for they thought to have seen that other, and they marvelled inly at the bravery of his suit, and at the horse, nor durst they ask him how he had come by it. And, when they counted themselves at the standard, one was missed from among their number, even he by whom the man had been wronged. And the man spoke them never a word.

Now, at the close of that day, it came to pass that the troop, with which the man rode, was drawn up where the Queen and her ladies had their stand; and, when the man beheld the fair beauty of those women, in all the glory of their jewelled raiment, shining beneath the royal canopy of blue broidered in gold, that was borne above them on staves of silver, his soul was stirred to admiration. And as he took up his allotted post he marked their laughter; nor was it long before he learned what cause they had to be moved so pleasantly, for the King himself, drawing up but a pace or two from where the man was, laughed also and waved his arm, so that the eyes of the man following that movement, saw that which had made them sport. And he beheld, in a space below, there where the dying sunlight touched the walls of that town, a woman,—one of those miserable ones, that fought, in her despair, with the dogs that would have snatched the child from her breast. And the man thought, "Of a truth, the devils in hell shall be more merciful than these!" And the laughter of the ladies was hateful in his ears.

And at that moment the prince marshal, he that rode on the King's right hand, marked the working of the man's countenance, and he noted his great stature and the fashion of that armour which he wore, and it was to him as if all these things were familiar to him. And he called to him the captain of that troop and said, "Tell me, who is he that rides with thee, mounted on a gray horse, and having arms of black and of silver, inlaid after the Italian fashion?"

And the captain made answer and said, "We know him not, nor will he reveal himself to any among us, and he hath ever denied me his name."

Then, said the prince-marshal, "Let him come up hither!"

And the captain went to the man and said, "It is the prince-marshal, he that hath white hairs and that rides on the right hand of the King, and he calls for thee, and bids thee go up thither, and declare thy name." And the captain said, furthermore, "He is that great prince and duke that beareth on his banner three dragons of gold on a field azure."

And, when the man heard that, he knew the prince to be he that had slain his father and had despoiled him of his inheritance, and he knew himself, also, to be fallen into his hands, and he thought, "Is it for this that I have come into the presence of the King!" And for all they called him he budged not, neither did he open his mouth. And he was become as one dumb.

Then that prince grew angry at his tarrying, and he cried out, saying, "Will he, indeed, mock me also!" And he commanded the captain that he should bring the man before him by force. But, hearing this, the man stirred not. And, when the captain laid his hand on the man's bridle, the horse, that had hitherto stood patiently, began to rear and to plunge, so that he could not lead him. And the captain, being in much fear of the prince, called the others to him, and, seizing the man by his collar, would have thrown him to the ground. But, as he did this, the man's doublet opened, and they all saw the thread of scarlet about his throat, and they remembered the dead, saying, "He hath kissed the hangman's daughter!" And they all were afraid.

Then that horse, on which the man sat, with a great bound, cleared a space about him, and settling down into a mighty stride, carried his rider from their eyes into the gathering darkness. Nor did any offer to stay his course, for all gave way before him.

As the man rode into the night that was now coming on apace over all the land, he would fain have drawn rein, only he could not. And when he saw before him dimly, as in a dream, the lines of St. Catharine's Hill, he would have dismounted, but his feet were heavy so that he could not lift them, and it seemed to him as if one pulled him by the heel. And being angered thereat, he strove furiously to turn his horse, but the horse was his master, and as he looked back over his shoulder he was aware of a gray shape that followed him swiftly from afar. And the darkness increased, and close at hand he heard the rolling of the great waters, as the tide came in along the shore, and he knew, of a certainty, whither the steed of the dead should bear him, for he was in the sand hills that were at the gallows' foot.

Now, no sooner was he come near, then she in gray touched his stirrup, and his feet were loosed, and he threw himself to the ground. And he seized the woman by the throat, saying, "What is this? It is thy doing, and thou shalt answer to me for it." And he shook her roughly.

Then the woman made him answer, and said, "Where be thine own sins?"

At this the hangman's daughter, hearing their speech, came down to them, and she took the woman by the hand, and said to the man, "Vex not thyself, nor us. It shall be well for thee. Come, step up here, once more, that we may dance together!"

And when he would not she was angry, and said, "Hast thou done my bidding twice, and, at thrice, shalt thou say me, 'Nay'?" And she stretched out her hand and twisted her fingers in the silken thread that was round his neck, and she drew him after her, and they danced together.

Then the soul of the man was filled with despair, for, as they danced in that thick darkness, he knew that she led him up to the gallows' foot, to that same place where they had supped. And, when they were come thither, she stayed her steps and let him go, but, as her feet touched the ground, on a sudden the corpse fires gleamed, and by their light the man saw where her cloak of scarlet parted about her breasts, and he saw in the opening that medal of his, that was his mother's gift, and he heard his mother's voice, saying, "The Lord be with thee, in all thy ways that thou goest." And he made as though he would have snatched it from her to whom he had given it. But she, crying out sharply, "Wouldest thou have again that medal of thine!" undid the clasps about her neck and threw the medal far from her, so that it fell into the sea.

And, seeing this, the man forgot all else, and having

marked where it fell, he broke from those his companions, and clambered to the high wall that was above the sea; but the women pursued him thither, and they hung about him, praying him that he should not cast himself into the water. And the hangman's daughter cried to him, saying, "With those boots of his, thou shalt surely drown!" And the sobbing of her that was in gray was most pitiful, for she clung to him as if he were dear to her, saying, "I have a charm! Grieve not! We will fetch it again, yea, we will fetch it again from the deep of the sea."

But, even as he doubted whether or not he should cast himself down from that place, the moon came above the towers of the besieged city, and, as her radiance filled the earth, the black shadow of the gallows fell upon the three. And the man looked upon the faces of his companions, and he knew them who they were. And fear fell upon him, insomuch that, crying, "The Lord be my help!" he cast himself into the sea. And, as he did so, the laughter of the hangman's daughter was louder in his ears than the rolling of the deep waters.

Now, on the following morning, when the tide had gone down, the body of the man was seen lying on the sands, near to St. Catharine's Hill. And they that saw it knew him and said, "Lo! here is again the work of the hangman's daughter!" for they knew that he had borne her sign. But, when they had opened his shirt and found it not, they marvelled, and beholding the fingers of his right hand, that they were closed, they made shift to see what might be within their grasp, and they looked, and saw that medal of gold which had been given him of his mother. And the priest that was with them, when he had read its holy legend, said, "Take him up, and carry him to a religious house, so shall he have Christian burial."

Now, his mother had no tidings of that his death, for no man knew his name. And she waited, ever hoping to behold his coming again.

The Triumph of the Cross

Quid haec, ad aeternitatem?

OF old time, the Saracens, coming from across the
sea, made their nests in the hill fastnesses, to the
west of a great plain on the southern coast, wherein a
Christian people dwelt. And at divers seasons they came
forth from the hills in their strength, and harried the
land, so that the Christians were vexed because of them.
At the last, they made bold to seize on the chief city of
that plain, which was hard by the sea, and they drove out
the lord thereof, and slew his followers, and laid waste all
that country.

In these straits the lord himself sought succour of
the princes of the marches of the north, but they denied
him, nor had he ever again come to his own had not a
maiden of great honour and wealth taken compassion
on him, for he was very comely. And she proffered him
good and not evil, saying: "If thou wilt be for me, then
will I be for thee; I and all that is mine, all the days of my
life." And that lord, having proved his own mind, knew
it to be towards her, and he gave her "Yea" gladly.

Now the ruler of that great monastery, which looks on the plain from the east, was of kin to the maiden, and, when he heard that she was wed, he practised secretly with her, and with the princes of her house, how they might enter in and drive out the Saracens, and restore the lord, her husband.

And on a certain day, when the Saracens made great rejoicings and took little thought for their foes, they that were servants to the monastery slew the scouts that had been set upon the hills, and he that had been lord, coming swiftly through the passes on the east, smote his enemies, to their entire discomfiture. They that escaped the sword took to their boats; as they had come, even so they sailed away, taking refuge again in the mountains of the west; but the chief were slain, and great was the slaughter, for not any were spared save one.

It happened that as he who had been lord of that country rode in the plain (or ever he had come to the chief city) he marked a high tower and well defended, standing in a pleasant place. And it was a new thing to him, so he made inquiry, and those that had gathered to him answered and said: "It is the pleasure house of a great prince amongst them. Yet this day, surely, none shall be within save women and children, for the lord himself is at the feast; only his wife shall be there, for she is in travail with child."

As they spoke thus, they were aware of one that looked forth at a window. Then those that were with their lord warned him, saying, "Of a surety the woman shall find a way to apprise her husband of our coming, for she is wise, and she hath power over the birds of the air, and all creeping things are her servants." And they said furthermore, "Let us slay the witch before we go hence, for should we leave her alive, shall not great mischief befall us?"

So they entered into the court by a little gate that stood open, and all them that they found there they put to the sword. Only the witch they slew not; for, when they had come to the place where she lay, and had drawn aside the curtains of her bed, she ceased that great lamentation and moaning that she had been making after the manner of women, and lifting herself she looked upon them, and, when she had looked upon them, she laughed right heartily, and she defied them, saying, "It is well done, oh, ye dogs! Slay now the mother with the child; for if my seed live, then thine shall surely die!" And she cursed them, and the lord that was with them, with a mighty curse.

At the sound of her laughter, the Christian princes were ashamed, so they left her; but as their feet were yet upon the stairs, they heard a cry, and the lord of that country, turning back, beheld a strange sight, for the witch was seated on a white throne that was in the centre of the chamber over against a fair marble bason sunken in the floor, and she had drawn her garments about her and her face was veiled, and on her knees lay the child of whom she had been delivered, and at her feet, by the steps of the throne, were two swans that were in the bason, and they did obeisance unto her. At this the man greatly wondered, but as he would have gone near, the silken hangings that were by the pillars on either side fell close and shut him out. And one, that was of his wife's kinsfolk, laid hands on him, saying, "What do we here? Tarry not, or the hour is lost!" So they set a guard over that place and they went their way.

When the sun had gone down, that lord knew that he had the victory, and he bethought him of the white witch, and, taking his servants with him, he went to the enclosed place wherein stood the tower. And, when he had come there, and had opened the door of the court, he found all the guard, whom he had set there, dead, and the entrance to the tower was closed. And, while he stood there in the darkness, pondering these things, the air was stirred by a low laughter, echoing along the walls. And they that were with him, hearing this and seeing the bodies of the dead, besought their lord saying, "Unless we make haste to be gone we shall be even as they!" So they took up those that were dead and carried them away to bury them, and the white witch was no more seen of men.

The lord himself had been fain to depart from that place, and ever after he was ill at ease, for in his ears he heard that saying, "Shall my seed live, then thine shall surely die!" Insomuch that, when many years had passed, and a man-child was born to him, his heart was shadowed by a great fear, for he remembered the words of the white witch, and he knew that the fame of her daughter was noised abroad in the land.

Now, the lord died, when as yet his child was young, and the boy dwelt alone with his mother, and her kinsman, the priest, that was ruler of the great monastery, had authority over him, and as he grew he became secret in all his ways. And it was so, that about that time, when he was well-nigh come to be a man, a grievous sickness fell upon him, and he lay for many days as one dead, and his mother watched him, and in the night watches she heard the voices of the darkness about his bed. So she listened in great fear, and she heard them say, "Brave shall he be, and in wisdom shall he go beyond his fellows;" and yet again they said, "He shall be unsurpassed of any for comeliness and stature;" and yet again, "All the works of the Devil shall he do." Then the mother forgot her fear and cried aloud, "Yet shall he see God! Yea! Even in these shall he see the Lord God!" And after this there was a great silence.

Whilst these voices sounded in the ears of the mother, he, who lay sick upon the bed, was in a dream, and in his dream it seemed to him that he came to a place of great shining, and looking to see whence the light came he was aware of a wondrous fountain of flame, and out of its midst there rose a tree of silver; many leaves were on its branches, but on one branch budded a single blossom of scarlet fire. Now the beauty of this blossom drew the man's soul, and he made to pluck it, but even as he stretched forth his hand he saw that both tree and fountain were defended by a golden snake, whose whirling coils, in ceaseless movement round the bason of fire, made marvellous flashing of many-coloured lights and sparkles in the air. At the first it seemed to him in his dream that when he saw this he was wonderstruck and somewhat daunted as by fear, but anon, he was so drawn by his desire that, waiting his opportunity, he put out his hand and seized the flower. On the instant the coils of the serpent were about him, and as he struggled in his agony he awoke.

And, when he awoke, it was as if the branch itself, which he had seized in his dream, lay clasped within his fingers: for his mother, in her fear of the voices, had laid upon his breast a crucifix of silver and of ivory, coloured wondrously, which had come to her from Spain. And, the fever of his sickness being still upon him when he woke, the crimson stains flowing from the wounds of Christ appeared to him as the glorious flower of his dream, and the crucifix was as the silver branch whereon it grew.

When his fever had passed away the man was still haunted by the vision of his dream, and whereas, of aforetime, he had been minded, forsaking all else, to bind himself by solemn vows to that brotherhood of which his mother's kinsman, the priest, was the head, there now grew within him a great desire to know the world and the fullness thereof. All that in which he had had his chief delight appeared to him an empty endeavour; his blood was stirred, and he cried, "Lo! the whole earth hath been given for an inheritance, and it is very good; of a surety the Lord hath not made man that he should dwell among the tombs."

Whilst the man was thus troubled, the spring came on apace, and soon there were on all sides signs and tokens of the gladness of that season, for the spring made heaven of the earth in those lands. And the man went forth and took his way to the pine woods on the hills. But the rejoicing of all things in those deep solitudes made him the more ill-content; for, though he was now of a settled purpose, he had as it were some fear of the priest, who had been in authority over him, so that he was loth to speak openly with him of that which he had in his heart. And in all those days he was harsher than was his wont with his mother, and very moody, so that his servants feared his face.

But it so happened one morning, when he had ridden out from his gates in the dawn, that—coming to the marsh places between the hills and the sea—he heard on a sudden the voices of a glad company. And he saw near to a giant pine tree, the branches of which made a deep shadow on the drifted sands, a band of youths, children of the brown fisher folk by the shore. These had put off their garments and were wading in a pool of water that lay at the edge of that shadow. Now this pool was as a clear mirror of the sky, and on the surface thereof were star-flowers of white narcissus, which had their roots therein. And when the youths gathered these fair blossoms they shouted for joy. And one, elder than those others, seeing his lord approach, stepped out of the water and bowed himself before him, praying that he would take at his hands the flowers born of the blue waters; and, as he bowed himself, the drops fell from his naked body like dew.

So the man stood for awhile looking on this child of the wind and sun, and as he looked upon him the darkness of his spirit left him, and he went from that place with a light heart and took his way to the monastery, wherein dwelt his mother's kinsman, the priest.

The road thither was strewn with the wrecks of an ancient time, and in the winter that way was ever desolate, but in these days the almond tree was in bloom, and the waste spaces were as a garden. And, when he was come to the path under the rocks on which the monastery stood, the man saw him whom he sought walking in the sun on a narrow way hard by the walls, which led to a place enclosed and sacred to Our Lady of Myrtles. So the man, leaving his horse with his followers, made haste on foot to overtake the priest, and he came up with him as he was about to pass within that enclosure, and they entered together into the shadow of the inner hedge of myrtles, and, finding there a stone seat roughly carven with holy emblems, they two sat down on it in front of the shrine.

Then the man told the priest all his mind, and that in no wise was he now willing to forsake all else and lead that life which had of aforetime filled his desires; and the priest was wroth to be thus set at nought, for the man had great possessions, and he entreated him sore with many words that he should change his counsel, but he could not prevail with him. Nay, the more he did entreat him, so much the more did the man harden his heart against him, and becoming weary of his much speaking he began to look upon the offerings where with the young men and maidens of that country had decked the shrine, and which hung upon the branches of the myrtles round about it; and as he looked he saw these words, "Mater Amoris," graven deeply on the canopy of marble which protected the sacred image. Even as he read them he heard a silver sound, as it were the echoing of many bells, dying on the air.

"Lo!" said the priest, "it is the passing of the daughter of the white witch! She, even she, hath wrought this evil! Cursed be he that hath hearkened to the voice of her abominations." So saying, he looked keenly at the man. But the man answered him never a word. And seeing that his countenance was very heavy, and that-his lips were shut, the priest waxed the more hot in his speech; insomuch that anger grew between them, and where love had been there now stood coldness that was like to be hate; and when the man went from that place he was aware in his heart of a great longing to look upon the daughter of the white witch.

The sleep of the man now ofttimes forsook him, and in the night watches he would spring from his bed believing himself to be called by that silver music which he had heard in the grove of Our Lady of Myrtles, but when he gave ear to it the sounds would pass away even as a breath upon the air.

Thus it was that, rising one morning very weary with the voices of the darkness, the man went out from the castle, and took his way through the town that was nigh to the walls thereof; and he passed through that ancient gate, men call the Golden Gate, that had been there builded of the heathen aforetime, and went towards the shore. There, finding a place of reeds, where it seemed to him he should be alone, he cast himself down upon the sand to rest, but the trouble of his blood gave him no peace, and his thoughts vexed him, and the stirring of the reeds was like much whispering in his ears.

On a sudden, at the full noontide, he was aware of soft footfalls near at hand, and turning himself he saw, coming towards him on the sands, a white mule bearing on its back a woman wholly shrouded in veils bordered with gold. She was seated on a leopard's skin; the silken reins on which her left hand rested were of scarlet, and as she came near she shook them, and the man heard a soft tinkling as of many silver bells. And, passing by him very close, the woman turned herself somewhat, putting aside, for a moment, the veils which were about her; so that the man beheld the fair honey colour of her locks and the clear violet of her eyes. And he heard her voice saying, "I have a message unto thee, my lord!" And, looking closer, the man saw beneath her breasts, which were as circles of snow, a golden girdle, and on the girdle were words writ in letters of light; and as he looked on them the man had a great longing to read them, and he knew that woman to be the daughter of the white witch unto whom was his desire, so he arose and followed her.

Now the tower in which the woman dwelt was in a place not far removed from the shore, so that the walls of that pleasure-house were plain in their sight, nor was it long before they came to the outer gates thereof. And, as they came to the gates, the scent of the hedges of box, whereby her garden was enclosed, was very strong, for the sun was hot, and as they were within that garden, the spring tide cry of the tortoise was heard above all things stirring therein. At the end of the hedges were marble steps reaching to the terrace whereon stood the tower, and near to the steps was a fountain shadowed by orange-trees, and all those trees were mirrored in the water below, so that the many-coloured fish therein seemed to swim in a cistern filled with golden fruit and flowers of silver.

When they had come to these steps, the man took the woman in his arms and, lifting her off the mule whereon she sat, he carried her within the tower. And when they were within the tower, the woman led him to the secret chamber, wherein stood the white throne, and on the steps of the throne were bowls of violets; but the scent of the shining blossoms that had been caught in her veil, as they passed beneath the orange-trees, was stronger than the scent of violets. Then, when they were come within that chamber, the woman unveiled herself before the man, and she was as a marvel in his eyes, and he worshipped her, for she seemed to him the most beautiful of all the works of God.

And the woman said to the man, "Lo! I have waited for thee many days, wherefore hast thou tarried? Behold! the scent of the passion-flower is on my lips; the breath of the south is in my nostrils, and I am clothed about with the fires of the sun! Give me, oh, my lord! of thy life-blood! Is not the gift of all pleasure in my hands?" Then the man answered her and said, "I am thy servant," and there were no more words between them.

Now the enchantments of the daughter were mightier than the enchantments of the mother, for she charmed all men with a great charm, insomuch that nights and days were all one to him that had his joy of her. And she knew him whom she had brought within the tower to be of the seed of the lord whom her mother had cursed in the day of his triumph, and she made glad, saying, "He is delivered to me for a prey." And when the man went from her on the morrow he was as one that had drunk strong wine, and his desire was towards the woman, and he esteemed himself much bounden to her for her graciousness.

And, in these days, he that should have been a priest became a mighty man of war, and he established his borders and stretched forth his hand in his strength over all that country. And the princes of the marches of the north, to whom his father had been subject, he made to be his subjects, and all men obeyed him. Yet though he dealt justly, he was very tyrannous, for, making court to the woman that was daughter to the white witch, he took of her cunning and also of her cruelty; but the praise of all men was his and the honour of all, as they that hated him feared him and kept silence. And his fame was great through out the world. But the woman was as one lying in wait.

Now it was so that when the man had stablished his borders he could not rest therein, being minded to drive out the Saracens and all their people from the mountains of the west. And he called a time of assembly for all the princes that were at his command, and when they were come he spake his mind to them, saying, "By the Lord God, it is our shame, and vengeance shall surely overtake us should we suffer the heathen to abide in the land." But those others were in fear, and they hung back considering how it might be.

At this the man waxed wroth, and he spake many bitter things and many hard things to them, and, taking from his breast that crucifix which his mother had given him in the day of his sickness, he swore a great oath upon it and said, "By the body of the living God! This thing shall be done, and ye shall be the doers of it!" And he constrained them; nor would he suffer any to depart thence till they had yielded themselves to his will; but all those princes went away murmuring.

Then his mother and the priest took counsel and said: "This thing shall be the ruin of all the land;" and they said, "Let us seek out a maiden for him to wife, so shall he abide with us in peace." And the mother spake to her son, saying, "I am well stricken in years. Take now to wife a maiden from among the women of my people, and she shall be to me as a daughter, and thy children shall make glad my knees." But the man, her son, gave no heed to her words, his thoughts being towards one unknown to her. Then the mother, taking this, his silence, to be consent unto her purpose, sent messengers privily into the land of her birth that they might seek out a bride for him who should be beautiful beyond the thoughts of men.

Thus it came to pass that one fair morning, when the man went forth from the gates of the tower wherein dwelt the daughter of the white witch, he saw, as it were, light moving on the hills in the east, and the shining of a princely company. So, turning to one that stood by, he spoke, and said, "Who is this that cometh?" and that one answered him, saying, "Knowest thou not? Of a sooth, it is thy bride that cometh."

Then the man remembered the words of his mother, saying, "My messengers are upon the hills, and they shall return, and in their company shall be a maiden of my people beautiful beyond the thoughts of men, and she shall be to thee for a wife, and to me shall she be even as a daughter;" and the man was right angry, for the enchantments of the chamber within the tower had sealed his sight.

Yet, when he was come to the place where he should meet that company, and had beheld the maiden, that she was exceeding fair to look upon, the man's heart was softened towards her, and he said, "Let be! That which hath been done, is done." And to his mother he said, "Lo! I wed me as thou willest, so shall there be peace between us." And he sent great gifts to the daughter of the white witch, saying, "Let it be well with thee; I shall see thy face no more." This he did, knowing that it should be no otherwise; but in his heart it misliked him, for he thought, "Surely her soul shall be sad because of this thing."

But she, who had been aware of his purpose against her people, had sent them warning, saying, "The hour is come! Fall now upon the Christians and destroy them at the time of the wedding of the bride." And she gave no answer to the words of the man, nor reproached him, neither had he any sign concerning his gifts; only in the night time, as he lay by his bride, it seemed to him that he heard the voice of the woman weeping by his bed, and the bride turned in her sleep, saying, "There are tears upon my face!" and she sighed deeply.

Now the feasting that was made at the wedding endured seven days, and it came to pass on the seventh day, as they sat at meat, and the princes of that company which had accompanied the maiden were about to make them ready to depart, the lord, her husband, called for white wine, that he might pledge them, and they brought him not white wine but red. So he called his cupbearer and said, "Did I not straitly charge thee to give me of the white? Wherefore now hast thou poured forth to me

120

of the red?" And the cupbearer answered him, "It is a marvel. Have I not drawn of the white, and behold the wine is red!"

And it was so, that even whilst he spake one entered in haste, crying, "I have a message! The sisters of the bride, yea, even her young sisters, are in the hands of the Saracen, and the strong man her father is a captive unto them!" And, as he ceased speaking, the voice of the priest was heard aloud, saying, "It is the work of the daughter of the white witch. Cursed be he that hath hearkened to the voice of her abominations." And coming near to the man he made as though he would have laid hands on him. Then that lord in his anger, and because his heart was sore within him, struck him who had been his master on the mouth; and the priest spoke in a clear voice, and said, "I see blood on thy hands, Iscariot, even the blood of the Lord's anointed!" And, so saying, he departed from amongst them, and bid all those that were there to follow him.

At this the princes that were brothers to the bride were troubled in spirit, and the mother lamented herself, saying, "The curse is upon us. In the day of feasting our house is become a house of mourning." And she wept, wringing her hands and making a loud noise, but the bride that was her son's wife arose, and coming to her said, "There are times and seasons. Hold now thy peace, mother!" And she said furthermore, "Let the hands of my lord, thy son, be strengthened in the day of battle!" And the man was glad because of her words, and looking upon her he loved her; but all those the princes of her house took horse and fled away hastily.

And the counsels of the priest prevailed, so that at the day of assembling, which he had set for those who were subject unto him, that lord was alone. No man stood with him, and all those whom he had constrained made ready to lift up their hands against him; and his heart was very heavy, for he knew not who had betrayed him. Yet not for this would he let go his purpose, and in the great pride of his spirit he renewed his vow, saying, "I and my seed shall perish; yea, and all this people shall perish, but assuredly the heathen shall perish with them."

Then was the whole land filled with blood, for the Saracens were many in number, and they took the lords of the marches of the north one by one-for every man being in fear for himself gave no aid to his neighbour—and at the last when they had despoiled these princes and had ravaged all their country, they descended into the plain, coming over the mountains of the east even through the ways by which the bride and her company had come. Now, the man, seeing that the hosts of the heathen should come by these ways, had entreated the priest, his mother's kinsman, that they of the monastery should open their gates to him and to his followers, so that issuing thence they might fall upon the Saracens as they were in the pass; but they would not. And the priest, remembering the blow that he had struck him on the mouth, mocked the man, saying, "How shall thine arm protect us? Is it not shortened by a mighty curse? Lo! Now is the day of reckoning. Get thee now to the tower and to the foreign woman; peradventure she shall make friends for thee amongst her own people." So at their coming the Saracens found a free passage and a secure place where they might abide, for they of the monastery welcomed them with gifts. And the princes, who were captains over them, sent and fetched all they of their people that remained in their ancient seats on the coasts, and settled them in the land; only the castle was too strong for them so that they could not take it, and the man strengthened himself therein.

And it was so, that for many months the lord, who had been ruler of all, was as one dead in the eyes of men; but he made himself ready, and when he was ready he offered peace to the Saracens, and all men were amazed thereat, for they remembered his vow. And the Saracens made terms, and the terms were that the man should put away his wife, by whom he now had a son, and take to wife the daughter of the white witch, and that he and they should divide the land. These terms the Saracens made with the man gladly because they feared him.

And, when these terms were made, the princes and captains of their hosts came in great state on a certain day to meet the man, for they trusted him and would have made sure the treaty that was between them. And the place of meeting was in a valley hard by the castle which the heathen in old time had enclosed with walls and set seats about it, leaving in the midst a space for their shows and games. And beneath the seats on all sides were chambers and passages, and there was a way, hollowed out in the earth, whereby men could come into that place from the castle unseen.

Then when all the lords and captains of the Saracens were within that place, the man gave the appointed sign, and he said, "Look to it. There is treachery, oh, ye captains!" and at these words the gates of that place were closed, and the Christians fell upon them and slew them every one. And when they had done slaying all those chiefs, whom their lord had given over unto them, they went out into the country round about and slew all whom they could find; but they brought in the woman that was daughter to the white witch, and took her before their lord that he might kill her with his own hands. But he refused, saying, "Show me first the wrong that she hath done." And they answered him and said, "She also is of their accursed race. Is it not enough?" And he answered, "It is not enough," and he let her go.

Then they that knew her treachery were right angry, saying, "This folly had not been, but that his desire were still towards her;" and the brothers of his wife were hot against him.

So it came to pass that the man fulfilled his vow. But this his great triumph and slaughter of the Saracens bred sorrow in the land and heaviness, for in all the ways were the bodies of the dead, and the people refused to bury them, saying, "Let them rot by the ways. Are they not heathen?" And the woman, whom that lord had spared, took of the seed of the dead and she made cakes therewith and gave them to many, saying, "It is an offering;" and all they that did eat thereof died; moreover, with the seed she poisoned all the wells so that there was an exceeding great pestilence.

And the priest, that was ruler of the monastery, seeking how he might avenge himself, stirred up the people and said, "How long will ye endure this tyranny and the bitterness of your days? Behold, the land is filled with dead corpses; there is death at all your doors! How long will ye give yourselves over unto your oppressors!" And he said, "Oh, ye fools and blind, know ye not that your lord hath bewitched you?"

When the man saw the anger of the people, inasmuch as his most trusted servants were sick of the pestilence, he sent his little son, with a safe escort, to ask help at the hands of those lords the brothers of his wife; but they refused him and said, "We will require the blood of all this people, and the blood of thy wife, our sister, at thy hands."

Now, the lady of the castle had eaten of the witch-bread and she died; and, because of the sickness, there was none at hand to bury her. So they laid her on a bier before the altar that was in the chapel that stood in the inner court of the castle. And as they carried her thither, a noise rose up from the plain beneath like to the coming of a great multitude; and the lord, her husband, looking from the walls, saw that the people were gathered together against him, and, riding at the head of all that people, he saw his wife's brothers and the priest, his mother's kinsman. Knowing, then, that there was no help of any, he caused the gates of the castle to be opened, and there he awaited their coming, standing in the entrance-way over against the bridge.

And when that people had come within the walls they seized the man, and they led him into the chapel, and brought him before the bier. Now, in the chapel were lights burning, and on either side of the bier were cen-sers of gold, out of which went up a thick smoke of sweet incense; and the bier was covered with cloths of gold broidered in silver. And when they had brought the man before the bier where on lay the body of his wife, they lifted the cloths that were thereon, and they parted the white linen of her shroud, so that he saw her face. And when he that had been her husband saw her face his heart was rent by a great anguish, and, forgetting all them that stood by, and the great peril of his life, he fell on his knees and humbled himself before God, crying, "The floods have gone over me! " And, as he spoke these words, fear fell upon all them that were there, and trouble, for the smoke of the censers became as a white cloud that over hung the bier, and in that cloud was the image of Him crucified. Then the man's soul was uplifted, as in the day of battle, and he said, "In the hour of victory Thou hast been nigh me, but in the day of my humiliation I have seen Thee face to face." And, as he stretched forth his hands to that vision, they that were near saw the holy signs upon them as of blood.

And the hearts of all those people were turned, and they said, "Lo! he hath seen the Lord God! " And they laid hands on the princes, his wife's brothers, and they slew them before the bier; and in their rage they would have slain the priest also, and would have destroyed the daughter of the white witch; but though they entered into her garden, they could not come at her, for there, where had been her dwelling-place, was a great column of flame rising, and when they sought for the priest he had escaped.

The Stainless Soul

IN a city, near to the gates of Paradise, there dwelt a
girl so fair and good that she was dear in the sight
of men and angels. And it came to pass that the angels,
coming day by day into the presence of the Holy Virgin,
to do her worship, spake of the girl that dwelt without
the gates. And the angels of the Lord spake in such wise
that she, blessed above women, arose from where she sat,
with the great company of her maidens, and prayed her
Son, saying, "Surely, this one also is of those that Thou
hast given unto me." So the girl was brought unto her,
according to her desire, and became one of those beloved ones waiting ever on Mary Mother in the gardens
of Paradise.

Now, even as the girl's soul was stainless, so were
the garments that were given unto her exceeding white
and dazzling, but she had no pleasure in them, seeing
that she was ashamed to sit in that glorious company of
Saints and Martyrs, deeming herself unworthy, and she
thought, "Shall not Margaret, and Catharine and Agnes,
in their glory triumphant, despise me, in that I, alone,
of all these, have suffered no wrong, endured no shame

for Christ's sake?" And, the Blessed Virgin, knowing the girl's mind, bade her return to earth, for a little space, that she might so fulfil her desire, nor enter into the rest of the Lord until she, also, had borne the Cross of Christ.

So the girl returned to earth and dwelt once more, amongst men, in that city without the gates, and her desire, towards Him Crucified, was strong within her, so that, even in her dreams, she saw ever before her that Martyr's Crown which should make her the more acceptable in the sight of the Lord and of His Saints. But the way of the Cross was not revealed unto her, and things harmful came not nigh her, for daily all men praised the loveliness of her virtue, and her ears were filled with smooth words.

Thus it was that when the time drew near that had been set for her to re-enter those goodly gardens, she became very heavy in spirit, and cried day and night to the Lord, saying, "Oh! dear Lord! withhold not from Thy servant the token of Thy Cross!" And the anguish of her spirit grew, and she went forth into the highways and byways; but to find the way of the Cross was not given unto her. And, at the last, when she knew that the allotted space had well-nigh drawn to an end, she closed her doors and sat within; her soul being full of sorrow, and she said, "Yea, Margaret and Catharine and all that company are as a reproach unto me! Are they not watching for me even now from the balcony of Heaven, and shall they not say, when the dawn cometh and I arise and go to them, 'Lo! it is even so. See now, how should Our Lord grant to thee the palm that thy hands are too weak to bear?'" And at this thought, the girl was loth to re-enter that blessed company which sat within the bower of the Virgin, and she beat her breast in the bitterness of her humiliation, for she said, "Verily, He knoweth best, and He hath found me unworthy of the way of the Cross!" Now, as the girl said this, it was late eventide, and, through the lattice of her chamber, she saw the lights of that city, wherein she dwelt, shining in the thick darkness, and she threw wide her windows, that she might look out upon the street. And, as she looked, she heard, in her ears, the noise that goeth up from a great multitude, and it was a murmur of much cruelty, of oppression, and of sin, and, on that night, this murmur seemed even as a call to her, insomuch that she arose, and, lifting her latch, yet once again, she went forth. And even as she crossed her threshold, she came, the Lord leading her, to where was one suffering grievous wrong at the hands of men, and there was none to help. Then, it was with the girl as if she would have gone to that innocent one, but, seeing that there was, set between them, a great foulness and mire of black and troubled waters, she drew back, for, looking on the dazzling whiteness of her raiment, she thought within herself, "How shall I stand face to face with my sisters in the garden, I, the stainless one, should I be thus defiled?"

On the morrow morn, the eyes of the girl were opened in the light of Paradise, and she saw all those the Saints, her sisters, coming forth to meet her, and she went on her way towards them, but when she drew near and beheld their faces, lo! they were all very sorrowful. Then, looking on herself, the girl was sore amazed, for it was so, that evil stains had overspread the exceeding whiteness of her raiment, and she knew herself to be defiled. And, in that same moment, she knew that she, who for love of the Lord Christ claimed for herself the Martyr's Crown, had even denied His Cross. And her head was bowed before the Saints.

Then said Margaret, "Oh! my sister, the sting of thy sorrow shall be sharper than any death!"

The Mirror of the Soul

IN a cleft between two mountains, a castle was set on high, at the gates of the East, so that all the travellers of the earth needs must pass it; and within its walls was great store of such things as are desired of men, and it was a house of pleasure. The voice of fountains was heard in the rose thickets of the gardens; the scent of violets and of jasmine was within its courts, and the doors were ever open to those that were fain to enter.

On a certain day, that was fixed for her bridal, the woman that dwelt in this castle rose early and betook herself to a secret chamber, and, having come there, she sat and looked on the face of her mirror, and, as she looked, she sang, and she sang as one rejoicing in her beauty. And when she had ceased singing, she said, "May I find grace in the eyes of my lord, for he is a man of men." And she sang yet a second time, and, at the second time, her song was of the coming of Love.

Now, the mirror before which she sat had been given to her by her mother, who was a great enchantress, and every day the woman renewed her beauty in its shining, and its shining was as the shining of the sun. For the crystal balls that were on the frame were filled with many-coloured light, and the story of Life and Death was written along the borders with seed of rubies and of pearls, and the woman held the mirror more dear than all else she had; and she possessed great riches. So when her song had its end, she looked once more on the image of her beauty, making the holy sign as she did so, and she drew an azure veil, wrought with many threads of silver, over the face of the mirror. This she did that so it might be defended from stain or hurt, for she feared lest the spirits of the air, passing that way, should behold themselves therein and trouble the depths of its shining. Then the woman went forth from that chamber, and, calling her maidens to her, put on the robes that had been made ready to her bridal; but when they would have placed the crown above her veil, she denied them, saying, "Nay, but my lord himself shall do that." Even then, they heard the sound of music in the air, and, looking forth from the windows, they beheld where the mists that hung upon the crest of the hills had parted at that sound, and, in the parting, they saw the coming of a troop of horsemen, and their spears were as shafts of silver gleaming through the mist. And two, the foremost of that company, rode with trumpets uplifted, and, as they came onwards, they sent forth a challenge of joy and gladness to the whole earth. And, as the echoes of that second blast died away, the mists altogether followed them, and the woman beheld her lord all glorious in armour that was of silver and of gold, and she knew the scarlet plumes of his helmet and the scarves of his following, and she turned herself about that she might make ready to meet him. So she went down into the outer courts of the castle, for she desired to await him at the gate; and when he was come, she would have knelt, but he prevented her; and taking from her the crown that was in her hands, he put it on her head and he kissed her.

Then she made him great cheer, and welcomed all his following graciously; and when they were come within her gates and he had put off his armour, she showed him all the treasures of her house: there was not anything that she kept back from him, and she brought him to her secret chamber, and she unveiled her mirror before him. And the man esteemed the mirror greatly, and beheld himself therein gladly. It seemed to him that he had never known himself as he was therein revealed; and they two had great joy of each other.

Now, every year, in that country, when the summer was at its full, men went out in the woods that were about the castle, that they might honour the blossoming of the pomegranate. For, like as the budding of the may, in its dewy freshness, is held sacred to the delight of youths and maidens in the springtide, even so, in the full heat of summer, should the flower of the pomegranate be held in reverence, for it is the flower of passion, and from its heart springs that liking that the man, in his manhood, hath towards the woman. Few, indeed, there be that honour this flower with a whole heart, for this is a matter of great virtue, but if any possess the secret, to him are all mysteries revealed; death and time are the slaves of its servants, neither can any shame or fear overtake them that worship this flower rightly.

Therefore, when the day came for the gathering of the flower, the woman made a stately festival, remembering the love she had to her lord, and his constant duty and service. And she bid all that were willing to the castle, that they might bear her company, and bring back the flower to her walls in triumph.

And it so happened that many came from afar at her request, and amongst these was one, a stranger, who journeyed in great state; and at her arrival all eyes were drawn to her, for the canopy of her litter was of blue and silver, and it was borne by four men, that were her slaves; and they were Ethiopians. Now this woman was the daughter of a mighty chief, whose lands lay to the north, and there was a feud of long standing between that chief and the man that was husband to the woman that dwelt in the castle. And though, in those days, there was no open strife between them, yet was their quarrel unappeased, and like a fire smouldering, the which, if but a gentle breeze do stir the embers, shall send forth great flames. Nor had that chief been willing to see his daughter depart on this her journey; but she would not be gainsaid. For she was angered by the fame of the beauty of the woman and of the great desire that her lord had unto her, and she hated her for all that drew to her the hearts of men, and her mind was set to divine the secret of the woman's power so that she might take her lord from her; and she knew that she could do this, were she but once within their walls, for she was skilled in all false magic.

When the baskets that had been borne with great ceremony into the woods were full of the gathering, they that carried them took them back to the castle, and they were set before the woman, in the garden hall, that she might distribute the scarlet blossoms to her guests. It was then that she, seeing the stranger woman that was amongst hem, and being herself a lady of a noble courtesy, took thought to honour her; and she sent to her a branch of many blossoms by the hand of her lord. And the stranger, who was as one lying in wait, looking on it, made fitting thanks; and the man, in the name of his lady, bid her welcome under their roof; and she stayed there, with all her following, many days. And when she had learnt the secret of the mirror she went her way.

The winter months now were come, and during the time of snows, when scarcely might anyone venture without the castle walls, word came that the mighty chief of the north had overpassed his borders with a great following, and was carrying fire and the sword throughout the land. This he had done at the prompting of his daughter; for after her return from the festival of the pomegranate, she had not ceased to upbraid him; and she said, "Are you dreaming or asleep that you sit idle? Now, even now, you may surely take vengeance on your enemy. He has sheathed his sword and has changed his spear for a woman's distaff." So her father called together all that would ride with him, and they were a mighty company.

They had thought thus to take that lord unawares, but his defences were sure, for he was a great captain. Men joined themselves to his banner willingly; and the snows had scarcely melted before the camp in the plain beneath the castle walls was full of those who had espoused his quarrel; and he himself, having made ready to ride with them, took his leave of the woman in her secret chamber. Together they looked upon the face of the mirror; and the man's spirit was strengthened by that which he beheld within its shining depths, for the love that was between these two was even as a rock that cannot be moved, should the waves beat upon it never so violently, for the foundations thereof are beyond sight. So the man rode on his way rejoicing, but the woman veiled her mirror with a heavy heart.

And she looked forth, and called to mind that May morning, when it had seemed to her that all the earth had hearkened with her for the echo of his voice, and he had placed upon her head the crown of life; and she comforted herself, saying, "He shall doubtless return, in the strength of his manhood, before the flower of the may is set for blossom." But it was not so, for the war, of which he had thought soon to make an end, drew itself out day by day. And, when the summer was fully come, she had no heart for the accustomed festival, but it so happened that, on that day, news was brought to her by which she was somewhat comforted. For a certain troop of horse, the best that were in the ranks of the enemy, had deserted to the army of her lord, and they reported great dissensions amongst the men of the north, so that the victory over them was assured. This, however, they did in obedience to the daughter of their chief and in fulfilment of her hidden purpose.

For when certain amongst the followers of her father found that the man, their enemy, was swift to overtake, ready of wit, and more to be feared in battle than he had been in the days of his youth, they reproached her, and they said, "Where is thy magic and thy skill to read the thoughts of men? She that dwells at the gates of the East is mightier than thou." Then she made answer to them softly, and, when she had wrought them to her mind, she plotted with them how they might take the man prisoner by treachery, and she said, "Should he be delivered into my hands alive, it shall be well with you;" and that company, which was called the company of the Black Spears, agreed with her for a great reward. And her schemes found the easier favour with them because they knew themselves to be in straits; for the man had so taken up his quarters that the way by which they would have returned to their strongholds in the hills was blocked by his forces.

Now, when that company had come into the camp, they sought their opportunity long time in vain, but, at the last, an evil fortune delivered the man into their hands. For those of the north, being brave men and desperate, rejected the peace that was proffered them, and, gathering all their strength, attacked their enemies, trusting by the suddenness of their onslaught to have forced a way of escape. But the man and his followers met them in the plain, and he said, "Since they will have no peace, let it be war to the death." And he bid his people give no quarter. So they fought from early morning till the dews began to fall; and, in that hour, the man, seeing that the moment had come when his foes might be utterly destroyed, called on those near him with a great cry and pressed forward, and the company of the Black Spears rode with him. And the ranks of the army of the north trembled at his voice, and their line broke, and they fled before the charge of his horsemen, and he pursued them in his wrath. Late into the darkness of the night, the men of the east pursued their flying foes, and great was the slaughter before any rested from pursuing, and being overtaken by the night, they did not return to their camp, but rested as they might upon the field.

On the morrow, when the clouds of night had rolled away, the men of that army knew their victory, but their hearts were heavy, for they knew also that the lord, their leader, had been betrayed into the hands of his enemies. For the company of the Black Spears, that had been with him in his last charge, when they had come up with a large body of the northern horsemen that had forced their way towards the hills, gave the signal, and on the instant the lord was surrounded. All they that would have defended him were slain, and he was borne down by numbers and carried off the field. These things they learnt from the trumpeter who had ridden by his side, and was found, by them that made search at dawn, still breathing, but not far from death. And he died, saying, "God help our lady in the East!" for he had ridden, also, to her bridal.

Not many days after, as that lady sat alone in the hall of mourning, there was a step on the threshold, and, looking up, she saw, standing before her, over against a pillar of white marble, one of the Ethiop slaves that had carried the blue and silver litter of the stranger at the festival of the pomegranate; and, when he saw that her eyes were on him, he made reverence to her with much humility, and said, "Oh, Lady, may I speak?" and she made answer, "Speak."

So he spoke, saying, "My mistress greets thee by me, and sayeth, 'The battle is thine and the victory is with thy people; but this advantage thou hast gained to thy hurt;' and, further, she sayeth, 'What wilt thou give me, that thy lord may go free?'"

At this saying, the bitterness of death overflowed her soul, for she knew that her mirror was demanded of her, but she made answer and said, "Go back to her whom thou obeyest, and say to her in my name, 'Lo, I am thy servant;'" and the slave replied, "Lady, I will do thy bidding, and, in seven days, I will be here again, that I may receive from thy hands the ransom of thy lord;" and, so saying, he went forth from the hall.

Then the woman, clapping her hands, called in those that were without; and she said, "How came it that you let pass unquestioned that slave that was here even now, so that he came in unto me without authority? "And they said, "We have seen no slave;" and she dismissed them, and they were all much troubled, for they thought, "Surely, she is distraught with much sorrow." She, however, knew that the powers of darkness were upon her.

So, rising from the place where she sat, she took her way to her secret chamber, and as she entered she saw the brilliant shining of her mirror even through the veil that lay above it. And, withdrawing the veil from its face, she gazed upon it in the anguish of her soul, for she knew that should she give the mirror to her by whom it was demanded, all that great beauty wherewith she was clothed would pass away with it, so that the eyes of her lord should be turned from her and that her place should know her no more. And, as she thought these things, the

139

sorrow of them was heavier than the parting of soul and body; and she cried out, "Is there no help, none?" And, so crying, she looked up to the cleft in the hills, through which she had seen him riding to their bridal; and the might of the love she bore him uplifted her spirit on wings stronger than the wings of the eagle; and she had joy of her giving, and said, "If it be well with him, it shall be well with me!"

And so, when the appointed hour was come, the woman gave her mirror into the hands of the slave that he might bear it to his mistress, and received from him the pledge of her faith.

Hardly had she done this when a sound was heard, from the plains below, as of the coming of a great company in triumph, and the woman, standing on the castle walls, beheld afar off the standard of her lord and the gleaming of his golden armour; and she put her hands before her eyes, for, at his right, she saw one riding, and the trappings of her mule were of scarlet and of silver. At that sight the woman went heavily, as one in slumber, and she left that place, and going down into the courts below, she stood before her lord as he entered at her gates; but he knew her not, neither was she known by them of her own household, for their eyes were holden. But the stranger that rode upon his right hand looked upon her to do her evil, and she saw that the glory of her beauty was departed, yet she feared her; so, calling to her them that had charge of the gate, she said, "How comes it that ye suffer such an one to trouble my sight in this day of rejoicing?? And she bid them cast the woman out. And they cast her out, but they marvelled greatly at this command, and said, "This is the first time that these gates have been shut against the desolate."

As the days grew to months and the months to years, the fortunes of the lord of the castle were as his wife would have had them be; for in all that country was no man so great in riches and in power. There was peace in all his borders, the chiefs of the north paid him tribute, and the fame of his justice, his honour, and his courtesy was as a fable in the mouths of men. Yet, though all things prospered with him, his spirit, at times, was clouded; and though he bore his part in the great festivals that were duly kept within his walls, he moved in them as one who dreamed a dream. And his followers, who loved him, lamented the days of his captivity, believing that his thoughts went back to them, and that their memory was bitter. But the burden that lay upon his spirit was not theirs to judge, for as the days went by, it seemed to him that when he entered the secret chamber and looked, with the one at his side, into the mirror's shining depths, something was missing that had been revealed to him, therein, of old. And, in the perfect loyalty of his love and faith, he took shame to himself, and his heart was sore within him. Then she, the stranger, seeing that he was ill at ease, strove by all her skill to discover his mind, but she could not, for her magic could not master the things of the spirit.

Now it came to pass that as she watched him, she gave less heed to her own ways; and one morning, as she stood before the mirror, seeing him in close converse with one unknown to her, she made haste to join them that she might learn their business, and leaving that chamber quickly, she carried with her, in her hand, the veil that should have defended the face of the mirror from the spirits of the air. And hardly had she descended the stair before they came, rejoicing that they might behold themselves therein. So, on the morrow, when she would have restored the covering to its place, she found the silver shining of the mirror defiled with grievous stains and rust. And hearing the footstep, at that moment, of the man upon the stair, she made as though she would have hidden it, but he coming behind her, swiftly, withdrew the veil. And he gazed long on the tarnished glory of the mirror, and as he gazed, the trouble of his brain grew; for after a while the clouds that overhung its depths parted for a little space, and he saw his wife wearing the robes that she had to her bridal, and the scarlet flowers of the pomegranate were in her hands, but she lay upon her bier, and the crown, wherewith he had crowned her on that day, was at her feet. Then, as the vision faded, the echo, as it were, of many voices chaunting, passed him in the air. And he would have spoken; but the words failed him, and, of a sudden, looking strangely on her who stood beside him, he rent the veil, that he had taken from her, and casting the pieces on the floor between them, went out from the chamber as one pursued.

She, then, put forth all her enchantments but they could avail her nothing, nor could she by any means restore the shining of the mirror, nor make whole the veil that had been rent in twain. And, during all that time, the man sat silent, and he was as one fighting for his life; but on the morning of the fifth day, when she would have renewed her arts by a more powerful magic, the mirror vanished, and, at this, she was in fear, for she knew that the end of her power was come. Even in that moment, the man against whom she had practised all this evil came to himself, and he knew her treachery, and remembered him of the woman that had been cast out from those her gates. And in this memory all things became clear to him, and he saw the cheat that had been put upon him, and knew that she who had been his wife had paid the price of his freedom with that which was dearer to her than life. Anguish, now, laid hold of his soul, and love, swifter to overtake than vengeance, drove him forth to seek her whom he had lost. So, leaving that false mistress to be dealt with by those that were his servants, he took his way thence towards that quarter in which he believed she should be found, for he called to mind that sound of chaunting and the direction from which it had been carried to his ears. And, as he went on his way, he refused his captains, who would have ridden with him, saying, "This errand is for me alone." But they watched him until he passed through the cleft in the hills above and was hidden from their sight.

Now, as he rode, grief and pity and love bore him company; and on the breeze from time to time there was carried to him the sound of that solemn music by which he was drawn onward. It led him ever farther from the haunts of men, and at nightfall he lay by the wayside waiting only for the dawn, that he might pursue his journey, for sleep was far from his eyes. And, as he followed the voices, his path went upwards, till at the last he came to a slope on the hillside so steep and slippery that his horse could serve him no longer, so, dismounting, he continued his way on foot. As he turned the shoulder of the hill towards evening, he came to the outskirts of a thick wood, and being about to enter, he paused and listened once more for those sounds that had been very clear that day in the dawning, but now were again lost to his ears. As he listened, he looked towards the setting sun, and, so looking, he beheld the great plain beneath him, and he saw, far below at his feet, the cleft through which he had ridden and the walls of the castle that had been his dwelling-place. Even as he looked, the sun set, and he made haste to follow his path; but the wood was thick, nor had he gone far before the darkness of the night came upon him; so he set himself down against a tree that he might await the rising of the moon, which was then at the full.

So waiting, the man, being sore wearied, fell asleep; but his sleep was troubled, for, ever and again, it seemed to him that he heard the tolling of a bell, and then the chaunting of the voices that he had taken for his guide. At last, the moon being up, her light fell on his face through the branches, and, on a sudden, he awoke. And when he awoke he knew not where he was, for, whereas in the darkness he had perceived naught but the thickness of the wood, the moonlight now showed him the path, winding through a little glade in the forest, and the path led towards an open space, wherein stood a white chapel, the windows of which were of stained glass, and in the windows were lights shining, and all round that space the trunks of the fir trees showed like silver columns in the shadows. And, as the man looked, that solemn music for which he had listened came nearer to him, and he saw, walking together down the path towards the chapel, a company of nuns. Their white robes were shadowed in black, and as they walked they chaunted that solemn measure; and when they had come up with him, he heard the words of their chaunt:

"The fairest flow'r of Love
On Earth may perfect prove,
     And yet in Heav'n be known.
With us, it grows to height,
But blossoms in the light
     Of our Lord Christ's White Throne.
Oh, winged and godlike gift!
Love can our hearts uplift,
     Until they meet His own."

As the nuns passed the man, one turned and, sighing deeply, beckoned him that he should follow, and he rose and followed them; but when they had come to the chapel, they parted from him, going towards the gate of the convent that stood hard by. But before they parted, she who had bidden him join himself to their company made a sign to him that he should leave them and enter the chapel; and he did so, and went up to the door.

As the man laid his hand on the lock his knees trembled, and his strength forsook him. He waited, as one in fear, till the sound of the chaunting had died away. Then, lifting the iron latch, he pushed open the door; and when it closed behind him he found himself alone with his dead. The woman lay on her bier, as he had seen her in his vision, clothed in the robes of her bridal, her hands filled with the scarlet blossoms she had loved; the crown of life was at her feet, but at her head the shining of her mirror made a great light of undimmed radiance.

At this sight a storm of passion and wrath swept the man's soul; and he cried aloud in the agony of his spirit, and it seemed to him, in his madness, that the gates of death must open to his hand. But the silence of the night gave back no answer to his voice, and the still shining, that was as the glory of a blessed saint about the woman's head, seemed to withdraw her from his arm. And, as the night wore on, wrath slept, and all that passion that had challenged fate fell prostrate, and the man cast himself upon his knees, and he stretched forth his hands as one that prayed for mercy. And, as he did so, the light above the bier became like the sun in its glory, and, within its secret fires, she, the Holy Mother of Sorrows, in her infinite compassion, revealed herself to his weary eyes, and her face was as the face of the woman whom he had loved.

When the morning dawned, the bearers came that should bear the woman to her burial; and the man, by whom the night watch had been kept, followed them with bowed head. And, when they had buried her, he took his way back to the world of men.

The Last Hour

A WOMAN, weary with long wandering in the ways of the world, came at last to the gate of the grave, and drew near to the steps that led up to it. And, seeing that it was close shut, she waited there for the Angel of Death, in whose hands is the giving of rest; and as she waited she turned herself about a little that she might look once more upon the glory of the earth.

The clouds of heaven were mirrored in the clear pool that was before the gate, and round about the pool were palms and aloes in blossom; and between their shafts and spires the woman, as she sat, beheld all the great beauty of the world. For a vast plain lay before her, stretching from the skirts of the high mountains, whose peaks were clad with ice and snow, even to where the southern seas were spread, glittering beneath the proud barriers of the earth. And the woman looked awhile on the majesty of the cliff that reared itself from the waters—rose-hued, purple-veined, tempest-riven, wearing the dark shadows of the woods as a crest uplifted against the infinite space of light and air.

And she beheld the ships that were upon those waters, both those that went down to the great deeps for merchandise, and those that men had made ready for battle. And from the waves of the sea, even as from the lands of the plain, there came to her ears the voice of life.

And, looking over the plain, she beheld the path of armies; the strong defences of the hills; the feet of the huntsmen that were towards the forests; the labours of the husbandman in the vineyard; and the presses running with wine and oil that were by the threshing-floors within his courts. And in the centre of the plain, above the blue vapour wherewith the evening, drawing nearer from the distant slopes, had begun to veil the earth, the woman saw a strong castle set on a little hill, and the walls and towers of that castle were shining in the last rays of the sun, and she knew from afar off the place that had been the place of her birth.

Beholding these things as she sat there alone, the woman remembered her of all the days of her life; and she said in the bitterness of her soul, "The spirit of man is even as a swift arrow that has missed the mark. For at his birth many are the gifts that are given unto him. He rejoices in the glory of his strength, and the eyes of men are made glad when they look upon him. The edge of his wit is as a sharp sword cleaving asunder things great and small, nor is there aught beneath the sun too wide for the compass of it. As his wit is, even so are his desires— strong in their flight as the wings of a young eagle. Yet nothing shall remain to him of all his striving, nor shall his strength have matched the height of his desires."

And the woman said furthermore, "Short are the days of life, and the strength of the body is a false servant to the spirit of man. Should his gifts be many or few, a bar is set that he may not overpass it. Lo! I am come to the gate of the grave, and are not these hands empty wherewith I would have handled all things? Surely, had I had my will, but one of all those of my desires, then had the infinite hunger of my soul been stayed!"

As the woman thought on these things, the shades of night drew on. The smoke that went up from the stations of the charcoal burners in the forests on the hillsides was blotted out. The white-winged vessels drew towards the harbour fires; the purple rocks, that were over against the sea, flushed scarlet as the sun sank beneath the waters, and all the murmur of the dwellers in the plain was hushed.

Then the Lord of the Spirit opened her eyes, and she saw as in a vision the souls of them that go down into the pit. And, looking on them, she was aware of the great multitude of such as had striven for mastery: amongst these she looked upon the company of those by whom Wisdom had been beloved beyond measure, and who had sacrificed to her possession all the joys of life; and there were those who had gathered to their own uses the hidden treasures of the earth and sea; and the luxurious ones, who had gone softly, and all those famous ones who had walked in triumph;—the armed men whose feet were dyed in blood. And, as she beheld them in that hour, they seemed to the woman as they had been possessed of madness, and it was as the madness of a House of Fools.

Then, said she, "It is well for me. Nor shall any deem himself as poor of profit, who hath tasted of the fullness of life in the sight of the Lord thereof." And, with this saying, she bowed her head in worship; for the Angel of Death stood before her, and the darkness of the night compassed them about even as with a shroud. The gates of the grave also were open. So she arose from the place where she had sat and placed her hand in his, and silently they drew within the tomb.

OTHER SNUGGLY BOOKS YOU WILL ENJOY ...

BLUE ON BLUE
by Quentin S. Crisp

A SUITE IN FOUR WINDOWS
by David Rix

NIGHTMARES OF AN ETHER-DRINKER
by Jean Lorrain

DIVORCE PROCEDURES FOR
THE HAIRDRESSERS OF A METALLIC AND
INCONSTANT GODDESS
by Justin Isis

BUTTERFLY DREAM
by Kristine Ong Muslim

GONE FISHING WITH SAMY ROSENSTOCK
by Toadhouse

METROPHILIAS
by Brendan Connell

THE SOUL-DRINKER
AND OTHER DECADENT FANTASIES
by Jean Lorrain

THE TARANTULAS' PARLOR
AND OTHER UNKIND TALES
by Léon Bloy

CPSIA information can be obtained
at www.ICGtesting.com
Printed in the USA
FSOW02n1059181016
26282FS